T5-BZP-817

Blaze™

Dear Reader,

Happy New Year! I hope that 2011 was kind to you and that 2012 promises to be even better. If you've picked up this book, then I hope that you've added "read more" to your list of New Year's resolutions. I always do and it's one of the few resolutions that I actually keep. Alas, it's the "diet" one that always falls by the wayside first, which is why my heroes always like a woman with a little meat on her bones. And the hero in this book is no exception.

Having been dubbed "the Phoenix" for walking out of a blazing building without so much as a blister, former army ranger Jay Weatherford has decided that it's time to stop tempting fate and presenting himself to the world of war as a perpetual target. But when Jay is tapped to find Truffles, the wealthiest Yorkie in the southeast, he's not altogether certain he's made the right decision. And when scrappy, smart-mouthed Charlie Martin starts getting in his way—and under his skin—he's absolutely certain of it.

As always, thanks so much for picking up my books! I am so very thankful for my readers and love hearing from them, so be sure to follow me on Twitter @RhondaRNelson, like me on Facebook and look for upcoming releases and news on my website, ReadRhondaNelson.com.

Happy reading!

Rhonda

Rhonda Nelson

THE PHOENIX

TORONTO NEW YORK LONDON
AMSTERDAM PARIS SYDNEY HAMBURG
STOCKHOLM ATHENS TOKYO MILAN MADRID
PRAGUE WARSAW BUDAPEST AUCKLAND

Recycling programs
for this product may
not exist in your area.

ISBN-13: 978-0-373-79661-8

THE PHOENIX

Copyright © 2012 by Rhonda Nelson

ABOUT THE AUTHOR

A Waldenbooks bestselling author, two-time RITA®
Award nominee and *RT Book Reviews* Reviewers'
Choice nominee, Rhonda Nelson writes hot romantic
comedy for the Harlequin Blaze line and other
Harlequin imprints. With more than twenty-five
published books to her credit and many more coming down the pike, she's thrilled with her career and
enjoys dreaming up her characters and manipulating
the worlds they live in. In addition to a writing
career, she has a husband, two adorable kids, a
black Lab and a beautiful bichon frise. She and
her family make their chaotic but happy home in a
small town in northern Alabama. She loves to hear
from her readers, so be sure and check her out at
www.readrhondanelson.com.

Books by Rhonda Nelson

For Karley, my sweet, beautiful niece who will no doubt be as scrappy and resourceful as the heroine of this book when she grows up. Love you, Karley!

1

CHARLENE "CHARLIE" Martin had known before she walked into this interview that she didn't have a prayer in hell of being hired by Ranger Security. She lacked a key piece of equipment—a prerequisite of sorts—that would have made her an ideal candidate for the job.

A penis.

Nevertheless, she'd had to try.

Upon seeing her, Jamie Flanagan had widened his eyes in unmitigated shock, Guy McCann had choked on his coffee, but true to his cool, unflappable reputation, Brian Payne hadn't reacted at all. Not a single ripple on the pond of that admittedly attractive face. She studied him thoughtfully and couldn't decide if she more envied or pitied his wife. Breaking that icy exterior undoubtedly was its own reward, but putting up the effort to do it on a regular basis had to be exhausting.

"You're a third-generation officer, Ms. Martin, and you've been with the Atlanta P.D. for a long time," Payne remarked, studying the résumé that had been thrust into his hands moments before. He looked up. "What has prompted the desire to thwart tradition?"

There were a multitude of reasons—she was sick to death of the boys' club, the constant need to defend the few promotions she'd managed to snag since she'd come aboard six years ago, the most important of which had been her advancement to detective. She'd paid for her so-called police pedigree with snide remarks and pointed, knowing stares every time she received a pat on the back for a job well-done. Though she had a few friends and had earned the respect of the majority of her coworkers, frankly, the constant struggle to prove herself had sucked the joy out of the job for her.

When she'd decided to leave the police department, she'd made two lists. One featured the things that she liked most about the job—the actual detective work, putting the details together.

Charlie had a knack for seeing things other people didn't see, for picking up on nuances that remained hidden to other observers. For instance, she'd noticed a tuft of cat hair clinging to Payne's leg, indicating he had at least one pet. Guy McCann had red-rimmed eyes and had missed a tiny row of whiskers on his chin. She'd be willing to bet he had a newborn. And Jamie Flanagan… Well, the pink shimmer of lipstick on his ear meant he'd more than likely gone home for a nooner on his lunch break. A twinge of envy shot through her. She hadn't had a nooner or any variation thereof in more than two years and the prospect of changing the current status quo was dishearteningly bleak. But now wasn't the time to be thinking about her uninspiring, dismal sex life. She saved that for evenings in front of the TV, a carton of ice cream in her hand.

As for the second list, it had showcased her options, her ideal future employer.

Considering Ranger Security was synonymous with "the best," it was her first choice.

A lost cause? Probably. She was neither an army Ranger nor a man, but thanks to a non-gender-specific name and Juan Carlos—their secretary—owing her a favor, she'd walked in directly off the street this morning. She'd had to—the least little bit of digging would have revealed that she was a woman and then she'd never have gotten into the "inner sanctum."

More man cave than boardroom, the space she found herself in was littered with high-end electronics, supple leather furniture, a kitchenette, a pool table and a beautiful view of downtown Atlanta. Though she'd passed each gentleman's office proper on the way to this room, it was clear that this was where most of their "work" was done.

As for "thwarting tradition"? She smiled. "I

prefer to think of it as thwarting *expectation,* Mr. Payne." She gazed mildly at him, silently communicating that her reasons were her own. Naturally, her family hadn't liked her decision, but… "It's time for a change."

A flare of admiration sparked in his cool gaze and she lifted her chin a fraction, acknowledging the respect.

"This is quite a résumé," Jamie Flanagan remarked. "You graduated cum laude with a degree in Criminal Justice from the University of Georgia, spent the first three years in a uniform then were rather speedily promoted to detective." He paused, still reviewing the résumé. "Several commendations," he reeled off, his tone even, speculative. "You teach self-defense classes at many battered women's shelters and college campuses."

She knew all of this, as she'd written it. Yet she nodded. "Yes. The women at the shelters are there because, typically, a man put them there." *Bastards.* She'd had a friend once who was in an abusive relationship and it had taken years to get her away from him. The physical damage was one thing—it was the emotional turmoil that was truly insidious. "They need to know how to defend themselves." Her lips tilted. "The college girls come for the free pizza, but it's a good age to reach them."

"Why are you here, Ms. Martin?" Guy McCann

abruptly wanted to know. "I'm sure Juan Carlos has told you that we only hire former military—Rangers, specifically." "You're wasting everyone's time" wasn't said, but hung in the air like an unwanted stench.

All righty then. They'd reached the nut-cutting part of the impromptu interview much more quickly than she would have liked. But she appreciated brevity as well, so be it.

"I'm here because I want a job, obviously. With Ranger Security." She looked at all of them in turn, gauging their responses. Payne was in lock-down mode, not betraying so much as a twitch. Flanagan's face was set as well, but a tightening around the eyes told her that it was harder for him to remain impassive.

McCann didn't even try to hide his expression and he might as well have said, "When hell freezes over."

"I realize that I'm not former military," Charlie said, because in for a penny, in for a pound. She had absolutely nothing to lose at this point. "But I think my résumé speaks for itself and I'm more than qualified to handle the sort of work you do here. Surely you could see the benefit of having a female agent on staff…particularly considering how many of your cases have married women associated with them," she added. A gamble? Yes. But she'd never been one to play it safe.

Jamie Flanagan stood a little straighter and a blush crept across Guy's cheekbones. Payne still didn't move, though the icy gaze he directed at her would have made a lesser person quail.

"That's not public information," Payne said, studying her with unnerving intensity.

"Neither are your eBay IDs, your private email addresses or your most recent physical exams, but I've seen them." It hadn't been nearly as difficult as it should have been, considering their line of work. Thanks to a cool little program she'd written herself, it had only taken a few keystrokes. She mentally snorted. Their firewall was a joke.

No longer trying to imitate a stone statue, Jamie leaned forward, a mask of incredulous shock on his admittedly handsome face. "You *hacked* us?"

Charlie merely smiled at him. "I like the pendant you've picked out for your wife for her birthday. It's quite lovely."

The three shared a significant glance—one that might as well have communicated "doom"—then Payne turned that arctic gaze on her. He did not smile. "Thank you for pointing out the flaw in our computer security, Ms. Martin. Clearly that is something that will need our *immediate* attention. That said, we aren't hiring at the moment."

At this precise moment, no, so it wasn't technically a lie. She seriously doubted Payne ever lied if he could avoid it—he wasn't the type. But, due to her computer reconnaissance, she knew they were looking for another agent and fully intended to hire someone within the next couple of weeks.

Just not her.

Her blood boiled, burning away the instant disappointment. For whatever reason, she'd expected them to be *smarter*. To be *better*. To see reason. To look beyond her breasts and give her a chance.

"Right," she said, her eyes widening significantly. She knew exactly why they wouldn't hire her and knew her tone, which carried an edge sharp enough to cut granite, told them so. She stood and extended her hand. "Thank you for your time." Graciousness had been ingrained in her, though she wished she could have suppressed the impulse. The niceties over, she turned and headed for the door. She paused at the threshold and threw them all a look over her shoulder. "Give my congratulations to Major Weatherford, would you?" she said, her lips curving with biting humor. "I'm sure he's going to fit in much better than I would have."

And with that parting shot—and the narrowing of Payne's pale blue eyes (a reaction at last!)—she turned and made her exit.

"WELL, HELL," JAMIE said, pushing a hand through his dark hair, his expression wavering comically between alarm and dumbfoundment.

Guy's lips twisted in irritation. "You've got the *hell*

part of it right." His incredulous gaze shot to Payne. "Do you have any idea what just happened here?"

That was what Payne was trying to sort out, and a strange tension in his gut, one that was distinctly akin to discomfort, wasn't helping. He knew they were perfectly within their rights to hire whom they pleased, and not bringing on a woman who'd had the nerve to hack into their computer system *and then tell them about it* was completely justifiable. In truth, he could have threatened to have her arrested but didn't see the point, because if she'd been good enough to get into their system, then she was good enough not to get caught. He frowned thoughtfully.

Impressive, that.

But knowing they were within their rights and feeling good about what just happened apparently weren't willing to coexist. He reviewed her résumé once again, mentally reexamining the forced interview, and came to a startling conclusion—the résumé alone would have gotten Charlie Martin in the door. Would they have hired her if she'd been a man? He didn't know. But based on the résumé alone, he would have granted the interview.

No doubt Juan Carlos had known that, otherwise he wouldn't have taken the risk.

Still…

"Juan Carlos," Payne called quietly. No need to raise his voice. He was certain the little Latino man was lurking just outside the door.

Looking equally guilty and put-upon, the office manager strode quietly into the room. "You called?"

Payne purposely let the silence lengthen and pinned him with his gaze. "If you ever do anything like that again, you're fired. Do I make myself clear?"

Though it should have been impossible for him to nod with his nose so high in the air, Juan Carlos still managed it. "Yes, sir."

Jamie gave an imperceptible nod, approving of this rebuke. Guy, on the other hand, clearly thought firing him *now* would be the better option. Other than being an occasional pain in the ass, Juan Carlos was a flawless employee, keeping the office running with a smooth sort of efficiency that made their lives considerably easier. Even Guy's, though he'd be loath to admit it. In truth, this was the first toe Juan Carlos had put over the line and Payne knew their office manager wouldn't have done so without good cause.

He wanted to hear it.

"I assume you owed Ms. Martin a favor of some sort?"

"I did."

"What for?" Jamie asked, his voice still strained. He settled heavily on the couch and snagged a packet of candy off the coffee table. He was an emotional eater, his wife liked to say.

Juan Carlos's thin nostrils flared and color raced across his cheeks. "I'd rather not say."

Guy's gaze narrowed, his temper barely in check.

"You lost that right when you brought her in here this morning. *Speak*."

A muscle in Juan Carlos's jaw jumped and the heat that had colored his cheeks had painted the rest of his face, as well. Seeing the usually unflappable office manager so unsettled was concerning.

He took a small breath and released a smaller sigh, seemingly resigned. "Six years ago I met a friend for a drink in a club downtown. There were a couple of guys at the bar who heckled us, but I didn't think anything about it. After a while, it just becomes noise, you know?" He paused. "Fast forward an hour later. I paid the tab, left the bar and rounded the corner." He looked at Payne and his mouth turned into a mockery of a smile. "Before I knew it they were on me. It was Charlie who came to my rescue," he said, almost wonderingly. A bark of dry laughter erupted from his throat, his gaze turning inward. "This little scrap of a girl felled those big bastards like saplings." He paused as Payne and the others absorbed his story. Irony lit his gaze. "Needless to say, I didn't go to her self-defense classes for the free pizza." He shrugged. "We've been friends ever since. You took a chance on me, knowing what I am," he said, referring openly for the first time in his many years of service to his homosexuality. "Big, bad-ass military guys like you. I came to the interview fully expecting to be shown the door. You surprised me. Was it so wrong to hope you'd surprise her, too?"

The discomfort in Payne's gut intensified. "We hired you because you were the most qualified candidate for the job."

"I've been the most qualified candidate for lots of jobs I didn't get," Juan Carlos told him. The phone rang and, looking profoundly relieved, he jerked his head toward the door. "I'd better get that."

Payne nodded and watched him go.

"Wow," Jamie said, exhaling a disbelieving breath. He passed a hand over his face and absently rubbed the bridge of his nose.

Not a trace of irritation remained on Guy's face. He pushed up from the chair he'd been occupying and ambled over to the bar, where he poured himself a shot of Jamie's favorite Irish whiskey. He winced at the burn, then cleared his throat. "I'll admit her résumé is good and her wading into a fight to protect a stranger is admirable…but does that make her the better candidate?"

Payne mentally reviewed Jay Weatherford's credentials and compared them to Charlie Martin's. "No, it doesn't," he said.

"Then we're agreed?" Jamie asked. "Jay Weatherford is better qualified?"

Better qualified to fit the current job description, yes, Payne thought. Still… He couldn't shake the pesky premonition that they were going to live to regret their decision. Charlie Martin's determined, resourceful personality reminded him strongly of someone else he knew—his wife.

2

FORMER RANGER MAJOR Jay Weatherford flicked the end of the match against his thumbnail and watched the tip ignite with a strange sort of fascination that was quickly becoming all too familiar. The strong scent of sulfur perfumed the air in his new SUV, where he waited the last few minutes before his interview with the founders of Ranger Security. He felt the heat glaze his fingertips as the match burned down, before resignedly extinguishing the flame with a low, fatalistic exhalation of air.

Despite the fact that he'd walked out of a burning building in Baghdad without so much as a blister—not a single singed hair—he'd played with enough matches since then to know that he would, in fact, burn. Why hadn't he then? When other soldiers who'd been within inches of him had suffered terrible, agonizing wounds?

He had no idea.

"A miracle," his mother had said. "Sheer dumb luck," friends had insisted. A "freakish set of circumstances," the doctors had concluded. Probably a combination of all three, if you asked him.

The incident had earned him the nickname the Phoenix and, though he'd admit it had a certain cachet, he wasn't altogether comfortable with it. How could he be, given the circumstances? When, for reasons he could never adequately explain, he felt as if his comrades had quite literally taken heat that was meant for him.

Improbable as it would seem, given his chosen profession, Jay had never given much thought to his mortality, but after that little occurrence he'd become distractingly, unhealthily obsessed with it. Though he knew it was unreasonable, he'd come to the bizarre conclusion that he wouldn't be so lucky the next time. And luck, he'd realized, that mystical, magical thing that had always seemed to rest on his shoulders and ensure that, whatever reckless situation he charged into, he would be safe, had gotten other people hurt this time.

It was unacceptable, horrifying.

Had he shared these thoughts with anyone? No. He had trouble enough admitting them to himself. Sharing them was out of the question, a fact that had extremely annoyed Colonel Carl Garrett, who'd ultimately recommended him to Ranger Security. In truth, he understood Garrett's frustration. When a career soldier whom the army had spent considerable time and money training suddenly announced that he wanted to leave, an explanation was surely wanting. But how could he explain something he didn't fully understand? He only knew that he couldn't do the job anymore.

And an ineffective soldier got people killed.

He couldn't have that on his conscience.

Jay glanced at the clock, then exited the car and made his way around the building to the front entrance. A cold wind whipped through the bare trees lining the streets and rattled the branches, sending a flock of birds into the pearly-gray sky. Winter's only purpose was to make one appreciate spring, Jay thought, huddling deeper into his jacket.

He pushed into the office into a welcoming wall of heat. He noted serviceable commercial carpet, quality leather furniture and a bit of high-end art. The desk was neat and tidy, suggesting excellent organizational skills. A small Latino man produced the obligatory smile upon his entrance, but it never met his eyes. They were cool and assessing and, though it was ridiculous, Jay felt that he'd already managed to offend the man in some way.

"Jay Weatherford?"

He nodded.

"I'm Juan Carlos, the office manager," he announced with equal parts long-suffering and pride.

"If you'll come with me, the triumvirate is waiting for you in the boardroom."

The triumvirate? That was an interesting way to refer to the bosses, though he supposed for the legendary Rangers it was as good a moniker as any. Jamie Flanagan, Guy McCann and Brian Payne were still the subject of battlefield and locker-room lore.

With an IQ supposedly bordering on genius, Jamie had the brain to go with the considerable brawn. He'd been quite the player until he'd met and married Colonel Garrett's granddaughter. Known in certain circles as the Specialist, Brian Payne had an unmatched attention to detail and cool, unflappable calm that had set a precedent new recruits were still trying to reach. Guy McCann's maverick style skated the thin line between genius and stupidity, but he possessed instincts that were almost providential and the man never failed to come out of any situation on top.

Individually, they were formidable. Together, they were a force to be reckoned with.

Though he'd never heard the particulars about why the three had left the military and started the security company, rumor suggested that an unsuccessful mission that resulted in the death of a dear friend had prompted the untimely departure. He could certainly understand that. The hardest part about his own impromptu career change was leaving behind the friends he'd made along the way. Battle created an unmatched sense of brotherhood, forged bonds that were, in some cases, stronger than blood. He mentally grimaced.

That had certainly been the case between him and his younger brother. To his regret, he and Carson had never been particularly close. With more than a decade between them, though, there hadn't been much time to form any sort of true relationship. Carson had come along a week after Jay's sixteenth birthday; a driver's license—his ticket to freedom—and then two years later Jay had left for college. After college came the military and he'd been home so little....

At least that would be something he could rectify now. His little hometown—Pennyroyal, South Carolina—was only a two-hour drive from Atlanta. Easily overcome for Sunday lunches and other family get-togethers, a fact his mother had gleefully pointed out when he'd told her that he'd be moving to Atlanta.

His mother had been too thrilled to wonder why Jay had decided to leave the military, and his father too tactful to ask. A blessing, that, since it was something he still hadn't managed to explain to himself. And, frankly, was in no hurry to. He suspected too much mental excavation would result in revelations he wouldn't be proud of.

Shaking off an instant sense of dread, Jay dutifully followed Juan Carlos down the hall. He noted two offices on the left, a bathroom and another office on the right before they arrived at what Juan Carlos had indicated was the boardroom. One glance inside the room confirmed what he'd suspected all along—he was going to love it here.

It was a grown man's playroom—big-screen, flat-panel television, comfortable leather furniture, a small kitchen equipped with a counter full of snacks, a pool table, various gaming systems and a bar. Only a topless model popping out of a fake cake could have made it better.

Brian Payne strode forward and extended his hand. "Welcome to Ranger Security," he said. Jamie Flanagan and Guy McCann, who'd been watching *Pawn Stars,* paused the program and made their greetings, as well.

"Thanks," Jay told them. "It's good to be here." He cast a significant look around the room. "Nice," he said, nodding his approval.

Jamie laughed. "This is where we keep all the stuff our wives don't want in the house," he said, settling back into a heavy recliner. He gestured for Jay to sit as well, so he claimed a chair. A certain form of camaraderie hung in the air, one that bespoke years of familiarity, mutual affection and respect. It was a comfortable sense of belonging, leaving him feeling immediately at ease and included.

Payne arched a brow. "You've reviewed the employment package?"

Jay nodded. He had and had to admit that the

salary and benefits were significantly more than he'd expected. He said as much.

"You'll earn it," Guy told him with a grim laugh. "We never know what sort of jobs are going to come through that door. We've had agents doing everything from protecting society debutantes to looking for lost Confederate treasure to escorting fertility statues across the country." He flashed a smile. "Rest assured, you are no longer in a war zone, but you are *never* going to be bored." A significant pause, then, "And your first assignment certainly falls into the—" he hesitated and that brief pause made Jay's stomach constrict "—*surreal* category."

Hoping he looked more intrigued than nervous— Fertility statues? Lost treasure? What had he gotten himself into?—he made an effort to school his features into confident curiosity. "What sort of surreal?"

The three men shared a look, then stifled smiles— that sure as hell didn't bode well, Jay thought—and it was Payne who was silently elected to brief him.

"I'm assuming you're familiar with Betterworth Chocolate?"

Of course he was. It was one of the premier candy companies in the United States and had been around for decades. Betterworth candy bars were sold everywhere and were so popular that the company had built several theme parks around the country, each featuring chocolate-themed rides and attractions. The simple branding and quality flavor had made Betterworth unequivocally successful.

"Yes," he acknowledged slowly, wondering how the chocolate company needed to use Ranger Security services in a "surreal" way.

Or *his* services, rather.

"I'm assuming even though you've been out of the country the better part of the past year you heard about Ms. Marigold Betterworth leaving the bulk of her fortune to her—"

"Dog," Jay finished, chuckling, struck again by the absurdity of it. He shook his head. "Yes, I do remember that. The news made it all the way to Baghdad. What's a dog supposed to do with— How many million was it? Two? Three?" He laughed under his breath. "Unbelievable."

"Five-point-three, to be exact," Jamie said. Something in his tone derailed Jay's train of thought and made him pause.

"That would buy a lot of dog biscuits," he said levelly. A dreadful premonition prodded his belly. A horrible suspicion took hold. Surely to God he wasn't going to have to provide protection for a *dog.* And not even a proper dog, if memory served. Not a Lab or a golden retriever. No, he was certain it was one of those teensy toy breeds women toted around in their purses. Delicate, fragile and of no practical purpose whatsoever.

"As you can imagine, the family wasn't pleased with the terms of the will."

He supposed not. He couldn't imagine that the pioneering members of the family that had started the company would have been too happy with the decision either, but who was he to judge? How people ultimately spent their money wasn't his business.

But he suspected how Marigold Betterworth had decided to spend hers was going to be.

Payne opened a file and handed it to him. "That's Truffles," he said. "The canine heir."

He'd been right. It was a Yorkie. Dark brown with caramel markings around its button nose and dark, inquisitive eyes. A pink bow sat perched between its alert little ears and a diamond-studded collar circled its small neck. A platinum tag in the shape of a chocolate truffle dangled from the collar and its name had been elegantly engraved in fancy script upon the surface.

"Yesterday, while outside for her regularly scheduled exercise, she vanished from the estate."

"Dognapped?" Disbelief washed through him. Definitely surreal.

Payne nodded. "A ransom note arrived within three hours of her disappearance."

This just got better and better. "Their demands?"

"Two million by the end of the week or they'll kill the dog."

A flash of anger made him scowl. Bastards. It

wasn't the dog's fault that her owner had left her with millions of dollars. In fact, given that Marigold had decided that the dog was more deserving than the family…what exactly did that say about them?

"Which, as bad as that is, actually tells us something about the dognappers," Payne added.

Intrigued, Jay levered a brow. "How so?"

"Because if they were familiar with the terms of the will they'd know that if Truffles dies of anything other than natural causes, the entire fortune—everything—goes to a variety of animal shelters across the country. The family will get absolutely nothing. Not a single red cent."

Wow. That was certainly one way to make sure that the animal was cared for. "And the family is aware of this?"

"That's who hired us," Guy said. "Andrew Betterworth, specifically. His sister, Taffy, is in Brazil on some sort of new age self-discovery tour. But, as you can imagine, they are particularly desperate for the safe return of the dog," he drawled.

Jay looked at the file once more. "Leads?"

Payne winced. "None, I'm afraid. No microchip. Mrs. Betterworth thought it was cruel. The collar was equipped with a GPS device, but it was put on a neighbor's dog as a decoy."

Jay glanced at the collar again. "I'm surprised they didn't find some way to keep it. It looks quite valuable."

Jamie snorted and absently scratched his chest. "Only if eighty grand is valuable."

Jay whistled low, stunned. "That's a lot of cash to strap to another animal."

"They've got bigger fish to fry," Payne said.

Maybe so, but that still seemed incredibly negligent. Who could afford to leave eighty grand behind? He supposed it was possible that the kidnappers hadn't realized how much the collar was worth, but common sense would tell someone that if an animal was worth several million dollars, then its bling wasn't going to be fake. Strange, that.

"Did you get anything from the note?"

Payne shook his head. "No prints, block-style lettering, delivered by a kid who couldn't give a description beyond 'old guy in a hat.' He gave it to the guard at the gate of the estate and said the gentleman had given him a hundred dollars for the job."

So basically, then, he had absolutely nothing to go on. No leads, no credible potential witnesses. Nothing. This was not good. Furthermore, Truffles's notorious fortune had made national headlines, which meant the list of suspects was literally limitless.

"What is the family's plan if we haven't found the dog—" he couldn't bring himself to call her Truffles "—by the end of the week?"

"Ultimately, that's up to Truffles's caretaker, Mrs. Aggie Tippins, Marigold's former head housekeeper."

Jay frowned. "That was an interesting choice."

Jamie shrugged. "Evidently Truffles liked Mrs. Tippins and vice versa. Marigold was confident that Aggie would take good care of the dog."

"You should start by talking to her," Payne told him.

That was as good a place as any, Jay supposed, particularly considering the circumstances. "I'm assuming Mrs. Tippins is the final authority on whether the ransom is paid?"

"Though there is a board of trustees and the lawyer, of course, yes, Mrs. Tippins will be the one to decide."

Jay reviewed a photocopy of the letter. A line emerged between his brows. "This doesn't say how the ransom is to be paid, just to simply await further instruction. What does that suggest to you?"

"Either a moment of opportunity presented itself or the kidnappers are very disorganized," Guy said, his shrewd gaze narrowing.

Exactly what he'd been thinking, Jay thought. He was going to need to talk to every person who had had access to the property and the sooner he got started the better. As this was his first assignment he wasn't keen on blowing it.

Though he couldn't say he was sorry that he'd left the military and gone to work for Ranger Security, he had to admit that had he known he was going to be searching for the wealthiest dog in the world— Truffles the freakin' Yorkie, for heaven's sake—on his maiden mission, he wasn't so certain he wouldn't have considered alternate employment. He appreciated the job—truly. But there was something quite... ignoble about it. It didn't have the same panache as "I survived hostile fire and avoided an IED," that was for damned sure.

Nevertheless, he'd signed on and he would deliver. He'd learned many things at the hands of his father—not to be afraid of hard work, that whatever was started had to be finished and how to treat a lady, just to name a few—but probably the most important lesson, the one that had served him the best, was to do what he said he would do. In fact, many of the world's problems today could probably be solved by people simply adhering to that code—appreciating honor, carefully, thoughtfully considering a commitment before making it.

Payne's cool gaze found his. "We realize that this is a different kind of work from what you're used to," he said, as though reading the thoughts straight out of Jay's head. "But we're providing a needed service, using our particular skill set to its best civilian advantage. Sometimes that's providing protection for visiting politicians, sometimes that's recovering kidnapped dogs."

Jamie grinned. "And the accommodations and company aren't half bad either."

Jay chuckled softly. "I won't lie and say that it won't take some getting used to, but that was going to be the issue with any new position outside the military."

Guy's expression was nonchalant, but his gaze was speculatively keen. "Colonel Garrett wasn't terribly forthcoming on why you decided to leave the military."

Smooth, but ultimately a lost cause. Jay merely smiled. Much as he appreciated his new career, he didn't owe them an explanation any more than he'd owed it to Garrett.

A loaded silence followed, then Payne broke it by handing him a laptop bag. "Here's your computer," he said. "It's equipped with all the software you'll need as well as interfaced with the programs we have here. Your gun is in there, as well as your permit to carry concealed." He gave him the code to enter the building and handed him a cell phone and set of keys. "To your apartment," he said. "Which is conveniently located in this building. It's stocked with all necessary items to get you started. Feel free to change whatever you wish regarding the decorating and whatnot. I just like to make sure that everything is ready for immediate occupancy. Typically there isn't a lot of time between being hired and setting to work."

Jay grinned. Evidently not. "Thank you," he said. True to his reputation, it appeared that Brian Payne had thought of everything.

A thought struck. "Where is the Betterworth estate?"

"It's in Asheville," Payne told him.

"Roughly a three-hour drive," Jamie chimed in.

Jay stood and expelled a short breath, then smiled. "I suppose I'd better get on the road then."

"Keep us apprised," Payne said, pushing to his feet, as well. "And if you need anything on this end, just give us a call."

Jay nodded and, assignment and objective in hand, made his exit.

"Never fear, Truffles," he muttered darkly under his breath. "I'm on my way."

PAYNE WAITED UNTIL HE was certain Jay was out of earshot and then turned and arched a questioning brow at his partners. "Well, what do you think?"

Guy chuckled softly. "I think he's wondering what the hell he's gotten himself into. Did you see the look on his face when you handed him the picture of the dog?"

Jamie's laugh was just as low. He rubbed his hand over the back of his neck and grinned. "That was priceless."

"You have to admit this case is a bit of a stretch, though," Guy conceded, kicking his feet up onto the coffee table. "Rescuing Truffles is about as far from Iraq as you can get."

No doubt that's what Jay Weatherford was thinking right now, Payne mused. "Be that as it may, Truffles is worth a fortune. There's a lot of money at stake."

He paused. "And finding the dog isn't the only problem he's going to have to deal with," Payne added, his tone ominous.

Guy and Jamie both turned to look at him. "That doesn't sound good."

"That's because it's not. I had a message from Aggie Tippins this morning when I came in. While the Betterworth family has hired us to look for the animal, Aggie has contracted her own help."

Guy's eyes rounded and Jamie leaned forward. "What?" they chorused. "But why?"

"Evidently Aggie isn't certain that the family's motives are as much for the welfare of the dog as they are about making sure their inheritance isn't jeopardized."

"I wouldn't argue with that," Jamie said, grimacing. "But who has she hired?"

Payne hesitated. "Falcon Security."

Guy swore hotly and Jamie, evidently disgusted, tossed what remained of his snack aside. While the new company hadn't undercut any of their business—though they'd tried—they'd certainly made a nuisance of themselves by plastering their flyers from one end of Ranger Security's block to the other. More than anything, the upstart agency was a pain in the ass.

"Dammit to hell—"

"Why on earth—"

"That's only the half of it," Payne interrupted

them. "They've put their newest agent on the case. Guess who it is?"

Jamie's eyes widened with dawning comprehension. "Oh, no. Surely you don't mean—"

Guy inhaled, his gaze darting to Payne. "The hell you say—"

"Surely, yes, gentlemen," Payne told them. "Aggie's agent is Charlie Martin."

Silence momentarily reigned as the three of them considered the implications of this news.

"She's going to be a nightmare," Jamie said, staring blankly at the wall.

Guy chuckled darkly. "A pissed-off, determined-to-prove-herself nightmare, to be more exact." He glanced at Payne. "Should we warn Jay?"

Payne shook his head. "There's no need. He's going to find out soon enough himself."

"So much for this not being a war," Guy remarked. "Something tells me Jay's going to be doing battle in ways he never anticipated."

Very true, Payne thought. And though he would never admit it to his partners, unbelievably…his money was on Charlie.

3

THOUGH CHARLIE IMAGINED this was a beautiful drive during the summer months when the leaves were in full display, there was something strangely creepy about the bare branches tangling together in a naked arbor along the driveway that led up to the Betterworth estate. It looked like something directly out of a Tim Burton film, she thought, glad when the bizarre gnarled arch opened onto a large pebbled driveway. The house was actually smaller than she'd expected, given the ones she'd passed as she'd drawn nearer to the residence. Her lips twisted. Of course, as she'd never been inside any multi-million-dollar homes, her mind had supplied Daddy Warbucks's mansion as her only point of reference.

And the admittedly grand stone manor house before her hardly resembled that. In fact, given the various vines growing up the facade and over the side portico, the home looked as though it would

be better suited to the English countryside. Smoke
even curled from three different chimneys along the
roof. A large fountain featuring frolicking nymphs—
naked, of course—stood in the middle of the mani-
cured lawn closest to the house, water burbling from
open fish mouths around the perimeter. Three red-
winged blackbirds sat on the edge in an odd little row,
evidently taunting a large gray cat that lay crouched
in the grass. The image made her smile.

Her back weary from the drive, Charlie pulled up
beneath the portico and shifted into Park. By the time
she'd reacl.., into the passenger seat to grab her purse
and her notebook—she still preferred plain old pencil
and paper to take notes—a man in a black suit had
opened the door for her. "Good afternoon, madam. I
assume you are here to see Ms. Aggie?"

Not accustomed to curbside service, as it were,
Charlie smiled up at him and nodded. "That's right.
I'm Charlie Martin, with Falcon Security." Though
she would rather have been able to say that she was
with Ranger Security, they hadn't wanted her, the
narrow-minded bastards. For an instant renewed
anger swelled within her, but she determinedly beat
it back. True, Falcon hadn't been her first choice, but
they'd hired her—given her the chance that Ranger
hadn't—and deserved her very best.

She fully intended to give it to them.

Though she'd been given a couple of small jobs—
to prove herself, she imagined—this was her first

substantial case. Yes, it was a dognapping. But this wasn't just *any* dog—it was the richest dog in the country and there were millions of dollars at stake upon its safe return. Operation Truffles couldn't be a more ridiculous name for this assignment—which was what the Falcon brothers had dubbed it—but there was nothing absurd about what the Betterworth family ultimately had to lose. Charlie desperately wanted to reunite the little dog with her caretaker and hoped that whoever had snatched the animal wasn't being cruel to it or worse, had already followed through with their threat to kill it. Miserable SOBs. Cruelty of any kind made her blood boil.

Charlie followed the gentleman through the large foyer down a central hall that led to a magnificent library. Floor-to-ceiling bookcases lined the interior, the woodwork a dark rich mahogany, deeply carved and beautiful. An enormous fireplace anchored one wall, a cozy blaze flickering in the hearth. Lots of poufy velvet-covered chairs were positioned around the room, plush multicolored rugs blanketed the floor and various globes and knickknacks added a certain lived-in atmosphere. The scents of cinnamon and leather hung in the air and the combination conjured a burst of nostalgia for her grandfather, for whom she'd been named. David Charles Martin had been a lifelong reader and had favored cinnamon tobacco.

He'd also been one hell of a cop and was the only one in her family who hadn't expressed disappointment when she'd announced her career change. He'd merely looked at her with those kind, wise eyes, asked her if she was certain—hadn't demanded an explanation or plagued her with why—and, when she'd nodded, that had been the end of the conversation. She inwardly scowled.

Would that it had gone so easily with her father, who still wasn't speaking to her.

When her older brother Jack had elected to join the military—ironically, *he* was a Ranger—instead of following the law enforcement path of their father, it was Charlie who Jack Martin, Senior, had turned to in order to continue the tradition. And she had, for as long as she was able to stand it. But she refused to spend the rest of her life in a career simply to appease her father. Life was too short for that.

"Ms. Martin to see you, Ms. Aggie," her escort announced.

Ms. Aggie, who'd been hidden behind one of the chair backs in front of the fire, turned and a relieved smile promptly slid across her rosy painted lips. She was older than Charlie had anticipated, with a wreath of snowy white hair crowning her head and cheeks that weren't quite plump enough to smooth out the wrinkles. Laugh lines were etched deeply at the corners of her eyes, suggesting a happy spirit and a willingness to find humor in almost any situation. Probably not this one, but... She wore a pretty pink fleece outfit with delicate embroidery around the collar, a pair of shockingly white Keds and reading glasses covered in daisies.

Charlie liked her instantly.

"Ms. Martin," she said warmly as Charlie strode forward to shake her hand. It was thin, but surprisingly strong. "I'm so glad that you could come on such short notice, but as I explained to your superior, time is of the essence."

"Of course."

She gestured for Charlie to sit, then turned to the gentleman who'd shown her in. "Smokey, could you ask Jasmine to bring a tray of tea and sandwiches, please?" She glanced at Charlie. "I'm sure you're hungry after the drive."

She'd actually gone through a drive-through on the way over, but didn't want to appear rude. "Thank you," Charlie said.

"It's no problem, dear. It's rare we have guests, so we all look forward to having company. I've had the Rose Room readied for your stay."

Charlie blinked. She hadn't been aware that she was going to be staying on the estate, had actually planned to get a room in town. She smiled uncertainly. "Er, I—"

"It's all settled," she insisted. "It'll be easier for you to keep me apprised of what's going on and, though I know you'll have to go off and investigate, it'll be best for all of us if you just make this your base camp. Though the family has hired their own detective, he'll receive the same accommodation. I thought that would be better," she said. "Perhaps the two of you can share information."

The more Ms. Aggie talked, the more confused Charlie became, and knew that her expression was one of frozen perplexity. "I'm sorry," she said, trying to hang onto a few threads of the conversation. "The family has hired their own detective? I'm not working for them?"

"Oh, no," Ms. Aggie said, as though the idea was unthinkable. "The family is only interested in the dog as it pertains to the money." She frowned darkly. "They don't have a care at all for what happens to my sweet little Truffles. That's why *I* hired you," she added patiently, as though explaining herself to a half-wit.

Oh.

Er…did Ms. Aggie seriously not see the flaw in her logic? It didn't matter whether the family had hired someone to find the dog because of the money or because of its well-being, they had still hired someone *to find the dog.*

The motive was essentially irrelevant as long as the goal was the same.

And the family was *highly* motivated.

Had the Falcon brothers known this? Charlie wondered. Were they aware that they were representing the caretaker and not the Betterworth family? For whatever reason, she seriously doubted they'd asked for the distinction. It certainly hadn't occurred to her.

And now not only was she going to be competing against another agent—*oh, goody*—she was going to be sharing a "base camp" with that person, as well. A dull throb began behind her left eye and she struggled to find her inner cheerleader to rah-rah herself out of this sudden funk of displeasure. She'd been here less than five minutes and already things were going to hell in a handbasket.

Not good.

But not insurmountable, she told herself.

Charlie took a fortifying breath and attempted to make her smile less fixed. "Thank you for bringing me up to speed, Ms. Aggie," she said. But now that she knew she was working against the clock *and* against another agent, time was of the essence. "Er... when do you anticipate the arrival of the family's representative?"

"Mr. Jay Weatherford here to see you, Ms. Aggie," Smokey announced from the doorway.

Imaginary doom music sounded in Charlie's head, her stomach dropped to her knees and her startled gaze instantly swung in Smokey's direction.

"Oh, do come in!" Ms. Aggie trilled, the epitome of graciousness.

The smile that slid across Jay Weatherford's lips was part aw-shucks, definitely sincere and unutterably sexy. It crooked endearingly at one corner, lifting just enough to make it imperfect but still intriguingly potent.

A strange flash of heat suddenly flared low in Charlie's belly and spread like wildfire through her veins. Her breath thinned, shallowed out until she could barely feel it moving between her lips. A dull roaring buzzed in her ears and the vibrations eddied through her nipples, which ruched inexplicably behind her bra.

She was so stunned she momentarily stopped breathing altogether.

Certain that he was welcome, he ambled into the room, his gait a...*drawl* for lack of a better description. It was unhurried, loose-limbed and confident. It drew the eye to his long legs and lean hips and beautifully sculpted torso. While she didn't imagine he spent every waking moment in the gym, he was definitely fit. The dark brown sweater he wore was loose enough to be comfortable, but still showcased enough bulk and muscle definition to make her mouth water.

But ultimately, it was his face that proved to be the most interesting.

It was rather long, his chin a smidge too sharp and his nose a bit too big. His eyes were a vivid memorable blue and fringed with curly, golden lashes. They matched his hair, she thought absently. Taken in parts there wasn't anything remarkable about his features, but together they made up a visage that was more rugged than handsome, more arresting than attractive. It was a face that compelled the viewer to more than look—to *study*—and that quality was as enigmatic as it was inescapable.

She was riveted.

He shook Ms. Aggie's hand and then hers—thankfully, she felt the blistering contact jar her to her mislaid senses—and continued to smile down at them. "It's a pleasure to meet you," he said.

For now, Charlie thought. But she seriously doubted he'd be pleased with her for long.

Impossibly, her motivation for finding the dog first had just climbed even higher. It was all she could do not to laugh maniacally and rock back on her heels because she could imagine no greater joy or satisfaction than besting Ranger Security's newest golden boy.

The one they'd hired *instead* of her.

And, oh, to be a fly on the wall when Payne, Flanagan and McCann heard about it.

"HOW FORTUITOUS THAT you've just arrived," Ms. Aggie enthused, her voice reminiscent of the Old South, where *four* was *fo-uh* and *supper* and *dinner* meant two completely different things. Her eyes were kind, her smile genuine and her hair was bright white and fluffy, putting him in mind of a dollop of whipped cream.

At her comment, the younger woman appeared to

smother a snort. His gaze shifted fleetingly to her, but that minute glance was enough to make his stomach tighten and his groin contract. She had a wide forehead, large curiously mocking hazel eyes, a small stub of a nose and a mouth that was plump and pillowy and curved into a perpetual tilt. Her hair was jet black, very glossy with a pronounced widow's peak, and it hung to just below her sharp little chin.

He was strongly reminded of a kitten he'd had as a boy, one they'd named Satan for its temper. He smothered a grin.

No doubt she wouldn't appreciate the comparison.

But she was quite striking, with her kittenish face and porn star mouth, Jay thought broodingly.

Part of the family? he wondered. Or part of the staff? He'd know soon enough, he supposed, but intuition told him the latter. Her clothes were nice, but appeared to be chosen for durability instead of fashion. She wore a pretty coral-colored cable-knit sweater that showcased a very lush pair of breasts, plain khaki pants that were quite wrinkled at the top of the thighs from sitting too long, and trendy leather lace-up boots, the kind with plenty of sole. Silver earrings dangled from her ears, a serviceable watch circled her wrist and her fingers were bare, even her nails.

If she were a Betterworth he'd eat his boxers.

"I'm glad I've arrived at a time that's convenient for you, Ms. Aggie," he said smoothly. "I believe my colleague, Brian Payne, called ahead and told you to expect me."

"Yes, he did," she confirmed. She gestured for them both to sit, then settled into her own chair, but before she could carry on, a woman bearing a tray of tea and sandwiches breezed into the room. The scent of roast beef suddenly permeated the air, making his mouth water. He hadn't stopped to eat on the drive over, had preferred to stay on the road.

The woman set her burden down on a foot stool at Ms. Aggie's feet. "Can I get you anything else?" she asked, her gaze warm.

"Oh, no, Jasmine, this is plenty. Thank you, dear." She quirked a delicate brow at her guests. "Refreshments?"

"I believe I'll have some tea, thank you," the mystery woman said.

Well, if they'd gone to the trouble to put together the sandwiches, then it would be rude for him not to select a wedge or two, Jay decided magnanimously. No doubt Kitty-Cat—he cast a glance in her direction—was watching her girlish figure or some such nonsense. In his experience, women were forever concerned about their weight, demurely picking through a salad as though it was a minefield, then falling upon the dessert at the end of the meal like starved hyenas. It boggled the mind.

Jay laid a napkin across his knee and helped himself, eliciting a smiling nod of approval from his hostess. "A man with a hearty appetite," she said. "I like that."

From the corner of his eye he perceived the slightest tightening of Kitty-Cat's jaw. Intriguing. Who *was* this woman? Had she eaten Bitch Bran for breakfast this morning? Or had he, somehow, without having ever met her before, managed to offend her?

He laughed softly. "*Hearty* is one way to describe it, I suppose," he said. "My mother always said she thought I had an empty leg to fill along with my stomach."

"Oh, I had boys," Ms. Aggie said knowingly. "I remember how much they could eat. I used to liken them to army ants, parading through the kitchen, stripping the fridge bare."

"Ms. Aggie, if you don't mind, I'd like to ask you a few questions about Truffles's disappearance," Kitty-Cat quickly interjected.

Though her tone was polite, Jay detected the slightest note of impatience. She withdrew a notebook and pencil from a bag next to her chair and flipped to a new page. A reporter then? That wasn't good. He'd been under the impression that the family hadn't planned to alert the media, that a host of false Truffles sightings would only muddy the waters and hinder the process.

She smiled then and the transformation of her face, the mere rearrangement of muscles, was instantly breathtaking. "The sooner I can start looking for your dear pet, the sooner I can find her," she said, her voice softening.

It was a nice voice—a bit smokey and melodic. It was so nice, in fact, that it took a moment to process the words she'd uttered in that lovely voice, but once their meaning surfaced, he was immediately confused.

And even more wary.

She was looking for the dog? But how could that be? That's what he was here to do. Clearly she was mistaken, but it wasn't his place to correct her. He cast a glance at Ms. Aggie, whose smile had gone sad.

The older woman nodded. "You're right, of course," she said, to Jay's amazement.

He laughed uncertainly. "With all due respect, ma'am, that's what I'm here to do, isn't it?"

"That's right," she said, nodding. "That's why I said your timing was fortuitous, dear. This way I won't have to repeat myself."

Though he tried to disguise his confusion, he was convinced that Kitty-Cat saw through him because, for the first time since he'd walked into the room, she looked as if she was actually enjoying herself. Try as she might, she couldn't quite squelch her cat-who-ate-the-canary smirk. At any moment he fully expected her to hack up a few feathers.

Rather than continue to delicately mine the situation one confusing question at a time, Jay turned directly to Kitty-Cat and extended his hand. "Jay

Weatherford, Ranger Security. I've been hired by the Betterworth family to find their abducted dog."

Her pointy chin lifted a fraction right along with her right eyebrow. Neat trick, that. "Charlie Martin, Falcon Security. I've been hired by Ms. Aggie to find her beloved pet."

She waited, presumably hoping he would ask about the redundancy of that. But if she thought he was stupid enough to point it out in front of their hostess, then Kit—er, Charlie Martin had another think coming. As the animal's caretaker, whatever information Ms. Aggie had was bound to be considerably more significant than anything he was going to find elsewhere.

He turned and offered the older woman a conspiratorial smile. "Two heads are better than one," he said, complimenting the logic his competition was hoping he'd fault.

She beamed at him. "That's what I thought," she said. "I'd hire another person, too, if I thought it would help me get my dog back. But as I explained to Ms. Martin only moments before you arrived, the family is only concerned with my dear Truffles inasmuch as the inheritance is concerned. Naturally, they weren't happy with the terms of Goldie's will and, to a degree, I even understand that." Her brow knitted. "But, particularly in Goldie's final years, that little dog—and the staff, of course—were more a family to her than anyone who shared her last name." She frowned thoughtfully.

"When her health started failing, they began circling like vultures, with their fake concern and solicitation." She looked up, a tinge of bitterness poisoning her smile. "They'd exhausted their trust funds, you see, and were actually having to work at the company that had afforded them their extravagant lifestyles." Ms. Aggie paused to take a sip of her tea. "Goldie saw through them, of course. It pained her that she hadn't a single relative who was interested in contributing to their heritage. It was her grandfather who'd started the company, you know," she added as an aside. "Even in her sickest, weakest moments, she still managed to give the company her best effort. She worked right up until the day she died. Most people don't know that. They just hear her name and think, 'Oh, that's that crazy old woman who gave her fortune to her dog.'"

She gazed unblinkingly at the fire. "She was so much more than that. And she appreciated hard work above everything else. She was generous to those of us who had served her well. She bought homes and provided extremely generous retirement packages to Susan, her personal secretary, to Horace, her gardener, and to Beatrice, her cook." She smiled again. "She gave me her most prized possession—Truffles. And a ridiculous salary as her caretaker, and this house." A soft laugh, then "She said I'd taken such good care of it over the years that I'd earned it. I don't know about that, but I do know that she was one of the kindest, most interesting and hardworking people I've ever known. She was never too good to do anything that needed doing, and never made anyone feel beneath her. We were happy to work for her, *wanted* to work for her."

Jay swallowed, touched by Ms. Aggie's description of her former boss. "She sounds like a remarkable woman," he said.

Aggie released a small sigh. "She was."

"A pity that her children were such a disappointment to her," Charlie remarked, evidently irritated on behalf of the late Marigold Betterworth.

Unnecessarily, though, as she was about to find out.

Aggie blinked, evidently baffled. "What children? Goldie didn't have any children. She never married."

Charlie's eyes widened in confusion. "But the family—I just assumed—"

"It's Marigold's niece and nephew—her late brother's children—who stand to inherit beyond Truffles," Jay told her, taking quite a bit of pleasure in it, too.

The look she slid him could have curdled milk.

Clearly she had not done her homework. And if she thought she was going to find the dog before he did, then she was very sadly mistaken. This was his first assignment for Ranger Security. Allowing himself to be bested by a rival agent from a rival firm was about as likely as rainbows and butterflies shooting out of his ass.

It wasn't going to happen.

And the sooner she figured that out, the better.

It was actually kind of cute, really, that she thought she could get the job done before he could.

4

"MR. WEATHERFORD IS quite right, dear," Aggie confirmed, much to Charlie's mortification.

"Jay, please," the object of her irritation demurred humbly.

Charlie *seethed*.

Aggie beamed approval at him, before turning her attention back to Charlie. "Goldie's father left a sizable amount of money to his son, Peter, but it was to Goldie that he entrusted the business. Peter was amiable enough, but a bit…dim, if you get my meaning. Anyway, Peter originally owned forty-nine percent of the company, but sold his shares to Goldie to help finance his son's auto-racing career. It never took off, of course." She grimaced. "Neither did his daughter's country-music career, for that matter, but it didn't keep Peter from trying, bless his heart. He died six years ago. Pancreatic cancer. He made Goldie promise to take the kids under her wing, to take care of them, and though Goldie tried, they wanted no part of her. They were too busy burning through what was left of their father's estate."

Given everything she'd just heard, Charlie was eternally thankful that she wasn't the one working for the Betterworth family after all.

She cast an arch look at Jay. "Your clients sound quite charming."

She caught a fleeting scowl of agreement before he could stop it and something about that one moment of shared opinion pleased her more than anything in recent memory. It was ridiculous, of course. He was The Enemy. And yet she couldn't deny the insane burst of pleasure, the warming of her heart, the sudden spike in her pulse any more than she could deny the air moving in and out of her lungs.

"We share the same goal, Ms. Martin," he said smoothly, then turned his attention back to Aggie. "I have every confidence that I'll find your dog before anything terrible happens to her," he said. So sincerely, in fact, that it took Charlie a moment to be annoyed at his gall.

She worked for Ms. Aggie. If anyone should be reassuring the older woman, it was *her*.

Charlie leaned forward. "Finding dear Truffles is my top priority, Ms. Aggie. I promise to have her back to you by the end of the week."

From the corner of her eye she saw Jay's especially sexy mouth twitch with repressed humor. So she amused him, did she? Well, he wouldn't be laughing long, the overconfident, unfortunately good-looking ass. He was so assured of his own success he didn't consider her a threat at all. She was so wearily used to this sort of mentality that she should be immune to it by now, and yet she found that she wasn't, that being discounted still stung. Particularly by him, which was as annoying as it was baffling, but there it was.

Ms. Aggie's face blossomed into another smile, her eyes crinkling predictably at the corners. "I am certain that, between the two of you, Truffles will be home where she belongs in no time at all."

Charlie's answering grin froze again. She sincerely hoped that Ms. Aggie wouldn't insist that she work with Jay Weatherford, though technically, as her boss, the woman was within her rights to do so.

"Of course she will," Jay said, managing to say the right thing without exactly agreeing with Ms. Aggie.

That was a nice skill. One that, admittedly, she'd never mastered. If she'd ever had a brain-to-mouth filter, it must have malfunctioned long before she learned to talk. Though she possessed enough tact to see her through social situations, constant effort was required to keep from saying precisely what she thought. Prevaricating didn't come naturally to her and, while she could recognize various shades of gray, her world—with her own personal code of ethics—was primarily viewed in black and white. She wasn't so stubborn that a well-reasoned argument couldn't make her change her mind, but those instances had been few and far between. She frowned.

Perhaps she needed more intelligent company, she thought, momentarily struck by the sudden notion. She blinked, forcing herself to focus. That was a thought for another day. Right now she had more pressing issues.

Like how to get some important answers out of Ms. Aggie.

"Ms. Aggie, I know that you went over the details of the abduction quite briefly with my boss, but I wondered if I might get you to recount the incident to me."

"I'm quite interested in that, as well," Jay remarked. "In fact, that's the reason I came to see you today."

"Of course," Ms. Aggie said. "I want to help in whatever way I can and am completely at your disposal." She paused, seemingly collecting her thoughts. "Truffles isn't exactly on a schedule around here, but I do let her out for a little while in the afternoon so that she can play. She likes to annoy the cat and frighten the birds and is forever digging holes in the flowerbeds, which annoys Mr. Hanover to no end," she added as an aside. "She's a tiny little thing, but is still a dog and enjoys doing the things dogs do. I let her out about two o'clock yesterday afternoon— it was right after her snack—and I had forgotten my knitting. I went back into the house, was only away for a couple of minutes, and when I returned to the backyard, she was gone. Vanished. I marshaled all of the staff and we searched for an hour before I finally admitted to myself that someone had t-taken her." Ms. Aggie's voice quavered.

"There's no way she could have wriggled under the fence?"

Ms. Aggie collected herself and shook her head. "The entire back of the property is surrounded by a brick wall. It's eight feet high and there are no gates. The only way in is through the front entrance and there are security cameras scanning that area all the time. In addition to having Burt man the front gate, an alarm sounds here in the house each time some-one enters the driveway."

And there was a lovely wrought-iron fence all around the front of the house, Charlie remembered. She'd noticed it when she'd approached the estate be-cause it was very elaborate, with curved branches and leaves and strange podlike features she'd never seen before. It had belatedly occurred to her that it was meant to look like cocoa trees. It was quite lovely and quite secure.

"So no one goes in or out except by the front gate?" Jay asked.

"That's right. Goldie liked her privacy."

And by controlling the access and limiting the points of entry, she could better monitor who was al-lowed in and who wasn't. She'd built her very own fortress here, Charlie thought. Modern-day, of course, and there was no moat, but it was a fortress, nonetheless.

So how in the hell had someone managed to snatch the dog in less than two minutes from a place that was seemingly impenetrable? Charlie imagined that scaling the wall could be done from the other side to avoid detection, but then how to get back over carrying the dog? Especially in such a short amount of time? She needed to get a look at that fen—

"I'd like to inspect the property, if you don't mind, Ms. Aggie," Jay told her, beating Charlie to the punch.

The older woman nodded her approval.

"Afterward I have a few more questions I'd like to ask you, provided you can spare the time."

"Of course, dear. Meanwhile why don't I have Smokey take your things up to your room?"

Charlie watched his affable smile atrophy and knew a moment of fiendish glee. *There you go, Boy Genius,* she thought. *Wiggle off that hook.* He cast a fleeting glance in her direction and, though she realized it was impossible, she had the distinct impression that he knew precisely what she was thinking, knew that she was relishing his discomfiture.

"That's most kind of you," he said, to Charlie's near slack-jawed amazement. She'd been certain that he'd refuse, that he'd insist on getting his own accommodation. "It will certainly make investigating a much simpler affair if I'm here instead of somewhere in town."

"That's exactly what I told Ms. Martin," Ms. Aggie said, evidently glad to have her logic validated once more.

Wonderful, Charlie thought, stifling the urge to groan. Now she looked ungracious. She aimed a slightly sick smile at him and noted the smug twinkle in those especially blue eyes. They were unpolluted by any other shade and reminded her of the morning glories that grew on the trellis next to her front porch in the summer.

Too late Charlie realized she'd made another tactical mistake—she shouldn't have looked at him. Because she couldn't seem to make herself look away. She was too busy puzzling out the various incongruities she saw there. Curly eyelashes in such a dramatic face, the almost lush mouth above his sharp chin. It shouldn't fit…and yet it did.

He was truly extraordinary.

Not the best-looking man she'd ever seen, but definitely the most appealing. At least, to her. Unbidden, an insidious vine of desire snaked through her, curled around her nipples and tightened deep in her womb. The sensation was so intense it stopped just short of being painful, left her shaken but hypersensitized, as though something long dormant had suddenly awakened.

With dawning horror Charlie realized it was her libido.

Oh, hell.

JAY WAS USED TO QUICKLY changing circumstances and was accustomed to having to modify his plans in a split second, so adjusting to being pitted against a rival agent and staying in the same residence as said rival agent barely registered on his radar.

If only he could say the same thing about *her*.

Somehow, in the mere span of fifteen minutes, she'd managed to become the most intriguing *and* most infuriating woman he'd ever met. To complicate matters even more, there was a constant sizzling awareness of her, a low hum of attraction that vibrated annoyingly along his nerve endings and, much like sonar, continually pinged his groin. His very blood *itched,* for lack of a better description, making him briefly wonder if he was allergic to her, but considering it wasn't an altogether unpleasant sensation, he didn't think that was the case.

He'd be better off if it were, that was for damned sure.

Being anything more than professionally interested in her was unforgivably stupid, insanely reckless and just plain ignorant. In truth, though he'd originally thought staying at the Betterworth estate was a bad idea, he was quickly able to isolate the advantages.

Furthermore, she'd expected him to balk, and

simply thwarting that smug little notion of hers held entirely too much appeal. She'd been waiting for him to object, had practically scooted to the edge of her seat in anticipation of it, the she-devil. The look on her catlike face when he'd done the exact opposite was something he'd likely enjoy for days to come.

But ultimately, staying at the Betterworth estate held multiple advantages, not the least of which was that he'd be able to keep an eye on her. Any lead she managed to get would be one that he'd get as well because that was obviously what Ms. Aggie wanted. He grimaced. The flip side was that he'd be forced to share, too. Nevertheless, he thought he had a better chance of giving her the slip than vice versa. His years of military training provided him a certain advantage, he felt sure, and he could evade and divert with the best of them. The old "friends close and enemies closer" adage would most definitely hold true in this situation.

Of course, it was the keeping her closer part that worried him the most, particularly considering this bizarre preoccupation he had with her. Had she been less interesting and half as attractive, no doubt this wouldn't have been an issue.

For instance, it would have never occurred to him to want to suck on her pointy little chin or feel her plain, unadorned nails digging into his back. He wouldn't have noticed the snug way her especially ripe breasts rounded mouthwateringly beneath her sweater or found the sleek curve of her jaw nearly as erotic. It wasn't so much the curve as the smooth, pale skin, contrasting deliciously with her hair. He wouldn't have taken any note of her long lashes or the shadowed crescents they painted beneath her eyes when she gazed at her little notebook.

For whatever reason, he liked that she worked in pencil, that she was willing to correct a mistake rather than scribble over it and start again. He'd always preferred a pencil, as well. A good old-fashioned number two, just like the one she'd been using. In fact, if he examined her too closely he imagined he'd find a lot of things he liked about her—beyond the obvious— and that was damned dangerous. He couldn't afford to like her. He had too much riding on this first assignment to blow it by letting the head beneath his belt take control.

With any luck, Ms. Aggie would put him in a room as far away from Charlie Martin as possible. No doubt he was going to need the distance.

FROM HER VANTAGE POINT in the library, Aggie Tippins watched Charlie Martin walk the eastern fence line of the front yard and, through another window, Jay Weatherford do the same thing along the back. She humphed under her breath.

"What's that noise for?" Smokey asked from behind her. His voice made something in her belly tighten and release, the feeling as startling now as the first time it had happened more than a year ago when she'd hired him.

"I'd hoped they'd work together," she said. She sighed and gestured out the window. "Clearly that's not going to be the case."

Smokey's chuckle mimicked his name. "Just because they have the same goal doesn't mean that they're going to work together," he told her. "They work for different agencies and for different people. They're competitors, not teammates."

She turned to look at him, struck again by the still-broad shoulders, the work-worn hands, the handsome lined face. "So it would seem."

"Yet you're disappointed." It wasn't a question. He knew how she felt, had had a way of peering right into her head from the day he arrived here.

Though Aggie had loved her late husband, they'd married too young, before either one of them had figured out who they were meant to be. Instead of growing up together as most couples did who had made the same mistake, she and Curtis had grown up and apart, like a tree with two trunks. Their lives had run parallel with a few common branches—their children, for instance—but, sadly, never together. Had they met even a year later she knew without a doubt that they would have never dated, much less married.

Did she regret her life with him? No, of course not. How could she when the very best part of her—her children—had come from it? And she couldn't say she'd been unhappy, because that wasn't true either. Aggie had never been one to count on anyone else to make her happy, so she'd never expected that.

But she could say that she'd never felt fulfilled, or even really understood. Curtis had loved her, just as she'd loved him, but it was an easy sort of love that hadn't demanded much more than common courtesy, mutual respect and the occasional obligatory night in the bedroom.

Smokey, though… He'd immediately understood her in a way that had been as terrifying as it was thrilling. One look into those dark, wise eyes and she'd felt laid bare and exhilarated, like a tightly budded flower opening for the first time.

He'd left her breathless—*breathless* at her age, when the idea of romance should have been a distant memory, a forgotten idea. He made her want things she'd long ago accepted were lost. She'd actually considered trying to manufacture a reason to fire him just so she could end her torment, but ultimately she could never bring herself to do that. She could never be that selfish.

"It would make things so much easier if they did work together," she said. "Two heads *are* better than one, which was part of the reason I hired Ms. Martin."

Smokey laughed softly, his low chuckle sending a shiver down the backs of her legs. "You hired Ms. Martin because you needed to do something to help bring that little dog back. You needed to act, to participate in finding her."

She smiled, acknowledging the insight. "True. But I also thought a different set of eyes would be good, as well. And the more eyes the better, as far as I'm concerned. She may see something that Jay Weatherford doesn't. Women often do, you know," she added lightly.

"I know you do," he said. A strange undercurrent in his voice impelled her to find his gaze once more. A beat slid to three, then he cleared his throat. "In any case, I think you've done the right thing," he said. "By hiring her," he added at her confused look. "Either they'll work together and find Truffles or they'll be so determined to outdo one another that you'll get more than their best effort and one of them will find her." He took a step forward, his gaze soft and earnest, and for a split second something passed between them. Something sweet and poignant. "Try not to worry, Aggie. It wasn't your fault."

Aggie's chest tightened and her eyes instantly watered. "That's a nice thing to say, even if it isn't true."

"It is true," he insisted earnestly. "It could have happened to any of us who took her out. Would you have blamed one of us the way you're blaming yourself?"

Probably not, she inwardly conceded, but it hadn't been a member of the staff—it had been her. And she'd managed to lose Goldie's most treasured possession, the little Yorkie that had become more dear to her than she would have ever imagined. It was strange how that had happened. She'd always been fond of Truffles, of course, but the dog had uncommonly bonded with Goldie.

Though she'd always heard the term "dogged her footsteps," she'd never witnessed it personally until Goldie had gotten the tiny Yorkie. Wherever Goldie went, Truffles had followed, and when Goldie had finally found herself confined to her bed, Truffles had stayed with her, curled up against her side. Aggie had been the only person who could get the animal to abandon her mistress long enough to eat and go to the bathroom. And Aggie had been the only person who could get Goldie to eat, as well. To outsiders she might have been merely the housekeeper, but in that final month she was a nurse as well, one devoted friend caring for another.

It was Aggie and that little dog who'd watched over their beloved Goldie, seeing her grow ever frailer and weaker by the day. It had been heartbreaking, one of the most difficult things she'd ever had to do, watching her friend move a little closer to death with every breath. But the shared adoration of their Goldie had led to a unique bond between her and Truffles and, when Goldie finally passed, they were left to grieve and endure together.

And they had, though it had been rough going the

first few weeks. Truffles had often whined at Goldie's door and routinely gone looking for her in her office, but the dog finally seemed to accept that Goldie was gone and had settled her affection solely onto Aggie. The comfort that loyal little animal had provided was simply…indescribable. There was something about feeling her nose nudging her hand, her silky hair beneath Aggie's palm that had made the world bright enough to keep looking for more light.

And now she had lost the little creature.

"Where would you like me to put Mr. Weatherford's luggage?" Smokey asked, interrupting her before she could sink further into despair.

"The Sapphire Room," she said, her gaze narrowing speculatively.

Smokey laughed again, the cheerful sound like balm to Aggie's aching heart, and she looked up at him once more and smiled. "They might not want to work together, but I'm most certainly not going to make it easy for them not to."

Admiration glinted in his dark gaze and clung to his grin. "That's crafty."

Aggie lowered her lashes and straightened her cuff, trying not to appear too pleased at the compliment. It was harder than it should have been. "I prefer to call it strategy."

His grin widened, further melting her heart. "You would," he said with a shake of his head, laughing under his breath as he turned and left the room.

Mercy, Aggie thought, feeling her heart rate settle once again into a more normal rhythm. *I'm too old for this.*

5

BECAUSE THE DOG HAD been nabbed from the backyard, naturally that was the place Charlie had wanted to inspect first, but considering Jay had infuriatingly headed in that direction, she had hidden her irritation—poorly, most likely—and made for the front. The entrance was just as she remembered seeing it from the road and driveway. Considering she was an even five feet, she'd decided that the ornate fence was double her height, with razor-sharp edges along the top. There was never more than a three-inch gap between the various wrought-iron branches, leaves and pods, and a quick check along the bottom revealed a two-foot cinder-block footer buried beneath the ground, making it damned near impossible to tunnel under, especially in the time it had taken to snatch the dog.

Furthermore, a careful look revealed scrupulously maintained sod and no evidence of excavation—attempted or otherwise—all the way around. Since the dog hadn't been abducted here, she'd expected as much. Still, she couldn't shake the nagging suspicion that she was missing something.

Certain that she'd covered every inch of the fence line, Charlie decided that she'd get the jump on Jay by talking to Burt, the gatekeeper, first. Even though her rival couldn't see it, she directed a dark look at the backyard and imagined her displeasure sending a cold shiver down his admittedly handsome spine.

It was petty to dislike the man on principle, she knew, and yet she just couldn't seem to help herself. Ranger Security had given him *her* job. She'd seen the recommendation from Colonel Carl Garrett, who'd enumerated all of Jay's finer points. Dedicated, self-motivated, a fine soldier, the special training—HALO, specifically—the multiple tours of duty, the commendations and medals. From what she'd read, Jay Weatherford had been the epitome of a for-lifer, the kind of soldier who planned to serve until he simply couldn't anymore. Charlie grinned despite herself.

Like her brother.

While she'd been playing cops and robbers and begging for rides in their father's patrol car, Jackson Oak (yes, named for the tree) Martin, Jr., was playing with army men and tanks. Their preferences were indicative of the paths they would choose, though admittedly Charlie had had little choice after Jack announced his intentions.

He was only two years older and they'd always been close. Out of courtesy, Jack had told her about his career plans before announcing it to their parents. He'd wanted her blessing because he knew the mantle of duty would shift to her and, initially, it was one she took up gladly to make him happy. She'd had no other real plans and, at the time, had been too concerned with pleasing her father and brother to object. And the kicker?

Even with hindsight, she wouldn't have changed a thing.

She'd learned a lot working for the Atlanta P.D. and was proud of her service there. But she would have never made her way around her father and grandfather's shadow and would have forever had the naysayers crediting any success she had to them, as well.

Charlie wanted to make her *own* mark.

She'd wanted to be the first woman non-military agent hired on at the best personal security company in the southeast—Ranger Security. She'd wanted to exceed the founders' expectations and garner their respect. She wanted to be appreciated, an asset, and judged solely on her ability and not by the accomplishments of her family.

And in the deepest, darkest corner of her heart, there was another reason as well, one she hadn't even realized until after she'd left their office, without se-curing the job.

She wanted a family.

Could she have had that and continued to work for the police department? Yes, she could have, she supposed. But watching her mother alternately biting her nails and checking the clock every time her father was late was something she didn't want to visit on her future spouse or children. Furthermore, though she knew there were men out there who wouldn't find her career intimidating—she had even briefly dated a couple—she'd yet to find one she wanted to keep around on a permanent basis. On some level it always became a competition, with her boyfriend du jour needing his ego stroked and her having to com-promise in order to keep him from feeling inadequate.

She was done compromising.

She wanted a man who was going to respect that she was strong, that she was intelligent. Those were good qualities, right? So why did they always end up becoming an issue? She wanted a man who was con-fident enough in his own right to go toe to toe with her, one who would give as good as he got, but who didn't constantly try to bring her to heel. She wanted mutual respect and admiration. An equal partner-ship. Strengths and weaknesses that balanced and were complementary.

Maybe she wanted too much, Charlie thought with an inward sigh, but if that was the case then so be it.

She'd rather be alone than compromise or settle and be miserable. She'd seen her fair share of friends do that and the outcome hadn't been pretty. One or both partners inevitably grew bitter and the people caught in the middle—typically the children—suffered the most. Charlie frowned. She'd certainly seen enough of that over the course of her career, and a steady diet of inequity was hard to stomach after a while.

Ultimately, that's why the job at Ranger Security would have been a perfect fit. It would have utilized her finer skills and renewed her faith in humanity. Furthermore, the firm was the best and she was just vain enough to want to be part of their team. Her lips twitched. Whose ego needed stroking now? Charlie thought. But there it was.

And it was that exact same ego that couldn't allow Jay Weatherford to beat her. She *had* to win, if for no other reason than to make Brian Payne, Jamie Flanagan and Guy McCann sorry for not giving her a chance.

Competing again—but the stakes, for whatever reason, felt much higher, as though there was a hidden purpose hovering just out of her grasp.

Irritated with the nebulous feeling, Charlie batted it aside and made for the guard booth. Burt, whose belly was large and hips nonexistent, was a mustached bald man with ruddy cheeks and no chin. He was playing solitaire on the computer when she arrived, but didn't start or flinch when she knocked on the door. A quick look at a second monitor indicated why—she was on-screen. As was Jay, crouched low, inspecting a line of fence along the back property line.

An arrow of heat winnowed through her at the sight of him, the sensation as thrilling as it was unwelcome. The way his jeans stretched over that especially mouthwatering rear end was criminally unfair, Charlie bemoaned, determinedly marshaling her thoughts toward something more productive than ogling her opponent.

Charlie smiled. "Burt, I'm—"

"I know who you are," he said with a long-suffering sigh. "I let you in here, didn't I?"

Her grin froze. That he had. "Right," she said, feeling momentarily stupid. "Could I ask you a few questions?"

"You can ask," he said, saving his game. "But I've already told everyone what I know. The story isn't going to change no matter how many different ways you phrase the questions."

Oh, wasn't he a charmer? "Be that as it may, I'd still like to ask," she told him, her tone leaving him with two choices—obedience or death. She'd run into her share of Burts over the years, the loudmouth braggarts who looked at her and saw a little pesky woman. She could lay his ass flat if she chose to do so and she'd had to cultivate a voice that conveyed that.

He looked up and reassessed her, then chose correctly. "What would you like to know?"

Now, that was more like it, Charlie thought, pleased. She wished she had a treat to give him. "Where were you when the dog was taken?"

"Right here."

"You never left the booth?"

"Only for lunch from twelve to one, during which time the gate is locked and the intercom system will buzz directly through to the house."

"No relief worker?"

He shook his head. "There's never been a need."

"And how long have you worked for the Betterworth estate?"

"Almost twenty years. I like being alone, so this job suits me quite well." No wedding band, she noted, and a cursory glance around the little booth noted a single cup coffeemaker, a mini fridge and several handheld video games. It was neat and tidy, but Burt had clearly made it his own.

Nevertheless, if Marigold Betterworth had been rewarding faithful employees, then why hadn't Burt been on that list? Had it been a case of out of sight and out of mind? Could he have taken offense at being essentially passed over while the others were given their just due? Charlie made a mental note to ask Ms. Aggie about Burt's status, then jerked her head toward the security monitor. "Is all surveillance recorded?"

Burt grimaced and shook his head. "Initially we were doing that, but with no incidents other than the occasional teenage prank, we stopped logging everything."

"What's your gut telling you on this, Burt?" Charlie asked, playing the old we're-on-the-same-team routine.

Predictably, Burt took a self-important breath and leaned in conspiratorially. "We are not alone, you know?" he said in ominous undertones. "They're out there. I've seen them."

A nudge of dread prodded her belly. "Seen who, Burt?"

She had her suspicions, but…

His nervous gaze darted hither and yon before finding hers again. "Them," he said significantly. "The other kind."

Oh, dear.

"I've been probed," he confided, then shrugged. "S'not as bad as everyone makes it out to be."

Alrighty then. Since she didn't have any idea how she was supposed to respond to that, she simply smiled.

"I've got some literature if you're interested," he told her.

"S-sure," Charlie managed, because to refuse would be unkind.

Burt grinned at her, revealing more gum than teeth. He opened a small drawer in the built-in desk—

one she fully intended to search as soon as he left for the evening—and withdrew a pamphlet and handed it to her. "We meet on Thursday evenings at the Pancake Palace and Tattoo Parlor."

Of course they did.

HOW IN THE HELL HAD they gotten the dog out of this backyard? Jay wondered again, genuinely baffled. Though he'd understood that the fence was essentially a brick wall with deep footers and only one entrance when Ms. Aggie had been explaining it, he nonetheless had truly expected to find the chink in the estate's defense, the point of entry that to an untested eye would be obvious once revealed.

He hadn't found so much as a blade of grass out of place.

He'd walked every inch of the perimeter several times, testing the ground and the brick, looking for evidence that anything had been tampered with.

He'd found nothing.

So if the kidnappers hadn't come through or under, then they had to have come over. But how? Better still, how had they gotten back over the wall without being seen? Without the dog barking or alerting someone that something was amiss? There weren't any trees or overhanging branches, so dropping over the wall from above would have been impossible.

Clearly a talk with the neighbors on both sides was going to be key, because from where he stood, he couldn't see any possible way someone could have entered from outside the property and taken the dog.

His gaze slid to the house. If, after further investigation from the other side of the fence, he still felt the same way, then whoever had taken the dog most likely had to be someone from inside the house. Someone that Ms. Aggie trusted.

Jay swore under his breath, anticipating *that* conversation about as much as a hernia exam. Somehow he didn't think Ms. Aggie was going to appreciate him suspecting the people in her home, the very ones he was certain she trusted implicitly.

But it wasn't his job to trust them—he was here to find her pet, and if that meant ruffling a few feathers, then so be it.

Even if those feathers belonged to Charlie Martin.

Hell, *especially* if those feathers belonged to Charlie Martin.

He didn't know what it was about the petite security agent, but she definitely had a way of getting beneath his skin. That perpetually sardonic smile, the knowing, superior look in those pretty hazel eyes. They reminded him of fall, Jay thought. Golden light, green moss and warm brown earth. Appalled at himself, he swore. Hell, he'd be writing poetry next.

"Watch your language," she said from directly behind him. "Ms. Aggie wouldn't approve, now, would she?"

Only years of controlling his impulses kept him

from starting. How in all that was holy had she managed to sneak up on him? His cheeks suddenly flamed with heat, and, with another muttered oath, he recognized the reaction for what it was—embarrassment.

She smiled up at him, her kitten face wreathed in a self-satisfied smile. "I hope I didn't scare you."

He fought a scowl. "Not at all," he said, turning his back on her once more. He inspected another section of wall, pretending that he hadn't already done so. Her scent reached him then, something bright and tart, like a green apple.

His favorite, damn her.

"Anything of note in the front of the property?"

She released a pent-up sigh. "Other than Burt the gatekeeper claiming to have been probed by extraterrestrial life forms and his weekly UFO group liking to eat pancakes while getting tattoos, no."

He stood and slowly swiveled to face her. The dark humor in her gaze seemed sincere, but he couldn't help wondering if she was just fucking with him. "Come again?"

She moved around him to get a look at the section of fence he'd been inspecting. She was much shorter than he'd originally realized. The top of her head barely came to his shoulder. "He gave me a pamphlet. They believe Jesus was an alien."

She got right up against the wall and started pressing her foot along the base, a single foot length at a time, looking for loose ground or a hidden hole. He'd done that as well, but had to admit he was impressed with her thoroughness. As a matter of fact, she seemed really attuned to her surroundings, her shrewd gaze skimming along the solid wall, looking for potential entry points. He liked the way she moved, too. Purposeful, with an economy of movement that was both graceful and seemingly unaware.

"I've done that already," he said, trying to save her some time. Which was ridiculous, when he thought about it. Every bit of time she wasted was to his advantage. *Note to self: be less helpful.*

"No doubt you have," she murmured noncommittally, continuing along in the same thorough fashion.

Because he was going to go along behind her anyway, he didn't take offense. Though he'd gone over every inch of this backyard very thoroughly, he lingered, reluctant to leave her alone. There could only be two reasons for this and neither of them appealed to him in the least. One, he was afraid she'd find something he hadn't, or two, he was unwisely intrigued by her. Disturbed, Jay realized it was both.

How galling.

Because that was simply…intolerable, Jay turned and made himself walk toward the front yard. He'd taken four steps when he heard her hum thoughtfully under her breath.

He stopped, closed his eyes and swore silently.

He retraced his path back to her side. "Found something?"

Evidently, she'd forgotten that she wasn't alone because when he spoke, she looked over at him and blinked. Then several emotions flitted across her unbelievably expressive face, chagrin being the most prominent one.

"Look," Jay said. "I realize that we're working for different clients, but the objective is the same—bring the dog home safely."

"I'm aware of that," she said tightly. A flash of irritation lit her gaze. "I'd just like to do it before you do."

He'd known that, of course, but hadn't expected her to be so direct. He rather liked it. He leaned forward, purposely invading her personal space just to test the waters, to see if she'd stand her ground or retreat.

"Once again, the same goal," he told her.

Her gaze narrowed. "Then you should prepare yourself to be doubly disappointed." She stood firm and lifted her chin, and the smirk that tilted her lips was knowing and a bit sad. He knew an instant of irrational regret, but squashed it with the reminder of what was riding on this assignment.

His job, his new identity, his livelihood…his new place in the world. He hadn't realized just how important those things were to him until just this second.

An inopportune moment for an epiphany, but there it was.

Jay hadn't recognized just how much he'd counted on being a soldier to define who he was, to give him purpose. Did he regret leaving? No, not really. He regretted that he couldn't effectively execute the job, that he'd walked out of that building miraculously unharmed when his comrades had been so terribly hurt. He could still hear their screams, the smell of burning flesh and singed hair, the agony. Bile rose in his throat at the reminder and he determinedly swallowed, forcing the images back.

Survivor's guilt, the shrink had said.

Whatever.

Just because it had a name didn't make it any easier to deal with. It was a label, nothing more. A point of reference for people who didn't have any idea what he was feeling.

And at the moment, he was feeling unreasonably infuriated. Because she'd found something that he'd missed. Because she was diabolically quick and intimidatingly confident. Because he was thwarted and angry and unaccustomed to this sort of insubordination.

But she wasn't his subordinate and he wasn't her commanding officer, and he had no authority over her whatsoever. He couldn't make her do a damned thing she didn't want to, Jay realized.

He watched the pulse beat rapidly beneath the pale

skin of her throat, her mossy irises narrow as her pupils dilated, her lips part for a shallow breath.

It took a moment for his muddled mind to connect her reactions into a single response, but when he did it was a game changer.

There *was* something he could make her want.

Gratifyingly, it was him.

6

THE SHIFT FROM IRRITATED to self-satisfied transformed Jay's face so swiftly that it instilled an inexplicable panic right into Charlie's rapidly beating heart.

She didn't trust that look. It...unnerved her.

"It's peanut butter," she blurted out, much to her instant consternation.

He blinked, thankfully, and drew back. "What?"

"On the wall," she said. She bent low and pointed. "It's only a smear, but that's what it is."

He joined her, his shoulder bumping hers as he lowered his considerable frame. She could smell him, too, something warm and musky with woodsy undertones. It did something to her insides, the combination of all that masculinity and scent made her middle feel gooey and her hands shake.

So, *so* unfortunate.

Him, of all people, inspiring this sort of unprecedented—she struggled to find a good enough word for this feeling and ultimately had to call it what it was—*lust*. Pure and simple animal attraction. He must have some truly potent pheromones, Charlie decided, barely managing to get her scrabbling thoughts back into order.

"You're right," he murmured, looking exceedingly grim that he'd missed it. He glanced along the rest of the wall and inspected the ground directly beneath the smudge. "No bird feeders nearby, so that eliminates that possibility."

"She was baited," Charlie said, pushing up once more. She looked from him to the wall then back again. "Give me a boost."

His distracted gaze swiveled to hers. "What?"

"I want to get a look at the top of the wall."

He continued to stare at her as though she'd spoken in a foreign language. Charlie exhaled heavily. "Fine. I'll ask for a ladder." She turned and started to walk away.

"No," he said, seemingly coming to his senses. "I was just under the impression that we weren't going to work together."

"We're not," she said, stepping into his laced fingers. She braced a hand on one brawny shoulder and resisted the urge to bite her fist. "But you're tall and time is of the essence. In this instance, it only makes sense."

That logic, she knew, didn't hold water. If it held

true here, then it was going to have to hold true at other times.

But she had something else in mind, so ultimately it didn't matter.

With a quick jump against his hand, she popped up onto the wall.

"Hey! What are you doing? Get down from there!"

Charlie held on tightly, then swung her legs over to the other side. "Okay," she said, shooting him a triumphant smile before dropping down to the ground.

"What the fu— Charlie!"

"Thanks, Jay," she called. "You saved me a long walk."

A fuming pause, then, "Well, what do you see?"

"Grass, mostly," she said, walking carefully along the fence line. She glanced from where she stood to the front of the property. There was no fence along the front lawn, so anybody wanting to grab the dog out here would have easy access. Along the sides, there was lots of tree and shrub cover, but there was nothing close enough for anyone to use to easily scale the wall. If someone had baited Truffles with the peanut butter—and she fully believed they had— then how the hell had they gotten her over the wall?

Curious as to what was behind the back fence as well, Charlie decided to head that way first. Strictly speaking, she was trespassing, but under the circumstances she imagined she could talk her way out of it in the event anyone approached her. She slipped behind various bushes and tree limbs, careful to look for disturbed ground or a missed clue. Other than a few scraps of trash she was certain had been neglected by the grounds crew, she came up empty-handed.

Damn.

"That was sneaky," Jay drawled as he rounded the corner, an impressed smirk tilting his lips. It was *insane* the things that little grin did to her insides.

"I like *efficient* better," she said, trying to suppress a smile.

He snorted. "You would." His thorough gaze slid from one end of her to the other, lingering along the curve of her hip and the swell of her breasts. "Not injured, I presume?"

Whoa. "From that little jump?" she scoffed. "Hardly."

"It's an eight-foot fence."

"And I'm five feet tall. Do the math, Ranger Boy."

A single brow lifted. "Ranger Boy?"

"You're a former Ranger, right?"

"That doesn't sound like a guess," he said, studying her more intently. Those keen eyes were capable of being much more direct than she would have liked and, for the first time since she'd met him, she saw evidence of a genuine opponent. He was affable, certainly, and charming, if she were honest…but he was a modern-day warrior, as well.

She'd do well to remember that.

"You work for Ranger Security," she said, moving around him once more. She wanted to check out the property on the other side of the Betterworth estate as well, just to make sure that she wasn't missing anything. "It only stands to reason."

Predictably, he fell into step behind her. "Maybe so, but my bullshit radar tells me that's not how you knew."

Perceptive. More so than she'd imagined. Another error in judgment she couldn't afford. "What does it matter how I knew?"

His voice developed a distinct edge. "Something tells me that's a key piece of information I need to have."

She pushed aside a branch and ducked behind another shrub, ignoring the strong impulse to flee. She'd be damned before she'd run from him. "You hear voices?" She tsked under her breath. "That's a bad sign. Perhaps you should talk to someone about it."

"You've proven that you're a smart ass," he said, clearly exasperated. "Now answer the question."

She picked up her pace, but his longer legs easily made up the distance. "You didn't ask a question. You stated your suspicions. Technically, I don't owe you an answer."

He laughed darkly. "Another purposely evasive answer, which means I'm right, otherwise you wouldn't be making the effort."

"Or I simply want to annoy you." She tossed a

wave at Burt as she continued on to the other side of the fence. "Have you thought of that?"

"You have no reason to want to annoy me," he said. "I don't know you and, ostensibly, you don't know me, therefore there's no past history to interfere with what should be a simple working relationship. That you clearly want to annoy me means that this is personal. And since I don't know you—have never heard of you until today—it only stands to reason that you do know me. Or at least *of* me."

She couldn't argue with that well-reasoned rationale, so didn't bother trying. With a huff of resignation, she drew up short and turned around to face him.

Only he wasn't right behind her as he'd been only seconds ago. He'd stopped several feet back and was inspecting something in his hand. Oh, hell. Now *she'd* missed something.

She backtracked only to watch him slide the mystery item into his front pocket. He smiled down at her, the wretch.

"What did you have there?" she asked. She'd told him about the peanut butter, dammit. Tit for tat, right?

"How do you know me?"

She blinked innocently at him. "I don't know you."

He chewed the inside of his cheek and appeared to be summoning patience from a higher source.

Irrationally, she got a perverse sense of pleasure from this.

"How do you know *of* me?"

He was going to find out soon enough, anyway, Charlie told herself. The instant he called in to Ranger Security to update his bosses on the status of the case he was certain to mention her involvement and the cat would be out of the bag, as it were.

At least this way she could enjoy his reaction. And she wouldn't have to tell him everything.

"I hacked into their computer system several weeks ago and saw your file," she said, lifting her chin. "Quite impressive. All-star pitcher at Pennyroyal High, ROTC scholarship to the University of South Carolina, completed Jump School at the top of your class, HALO training." She reeled off the majority of what she'd read and watched his expression slowly atrophy.

She wasn't sure if he was more angry or appalled, but his displeasure practically thundered off him like lightning off pavement. He'd gone white around the mouth and, though she knew she must have imagined it, she thought she caught a fleeting glimpse of fear lighting his blistering, mad-as-hell gaze. But that couldn't have been right. What did he have to be afraid of? What secret was he afraid she'd uncovered?

She'd gone too far, she knew, but was too proud to admit any contrition. In her experience, when she gave a guy an inch, he'd take a mile. And she instinctively knew that any ground she lost with Jay Weatherford was going to be doubly hard to regain. Still, something about his expression—that single look of vulnerability—haunted her, gave her pause.

He glared at her for what felt like an eternity, then turned abruptly on his heel and left without saying another word.

"DID YOU KNOW?" JAY asked Payne without preamble when his new boss answered the phone.

A significant, telling pause ensued.

Jay swore and sat heavily on his bed.

"You've met her already?" Payne asked.

Admittedly, he was new to the job and unfamiliar with the rules, but this was bullshit. Payne was his boss, not his commanding officer, and if the former Ranger expected blind obedience, then clearly he'd hired the wrong man.

She'd read his file.

He didn't have a fucking clue what was in the damned file, but given the level of expertise Ranger Security was known for, he couldn't imagine that it was anything less than thorough.

He mentally recoiled at the thought, his anger detonating once more. Since he was likely going to get fired anyhow he saw no reason to hold his tongue. Not that he would have been able to do so, anyway, but…

He flicked a match against his finger, watched the

tip ignite. "Look, Payne, I realize that I am low man on the totem pole here and that puts me at the bottom of the pecking order, but sending me over here blind when she was armed with everything in my friggin' file was *not* cool. I don't mind having to work around her—that's part of the nature of this particular assignment. What I do mind is her knowing everything from where I went to high school to my blood pressure reading on my last health exam and no one warning me about her." He blew out the flame before it could burn his fingers. "It's bullshit and bad form and I damned sure don't appreciate it."

He should probably quit before they fired him, Jay thought. That would be better than getting sacked, but leaving the military had felt too much like quitting, and the idea of this not panning out as well was damned difficult to stomach.

"You are absolutely right," Payne said, to his immense surprise. "I take full responsibility. It was my mistake. Guy actually suggested giving you a warning, but I failed to consider that she'd looked at your file when she hacked into our system and I didn't think that it was strictly necessary. Mea culpa, Jay. I'm terribly sorry."

While he was still exceedingly annoyed, it was hard to cling to his anger when faced with such a sincere apology. Particularly one issued from the Specialist. "I'm assuming the security breach has been rectified?" he asked.

"It was once she brought it to our attention."

He processed that, his mind sharpening into better focus. "You didn't know she'd been in until she told you?"

"No," Payne admitted. "She was careful."

Careful, hell. She was damned good. Hacking was one thing—hacking without leaving a discernable trail or evidence was another. That took a very advanced degree of skill. And nerve. "I'm going to want to see that file, Payne. I need to know what she knows."

"Understandable. I'll forward it right away."

Jay passed a weary hand over his face. "Thanks. I'd appreciate it."

"Listen," Payne said. "I know that she was disappointed that we hired you instead of her, but ultimately we all agreed that you were the better candidate for the job. She's impressive, I'll admit that, but—"

Jay stilled like a hound going on point. "What do you mean 'hired me instead of her'? You mean she applied for the position that I've got?"

"Yes," Payne said, sounding a bit baffled. "I thought that's what—"

"Oh," Jay said, his voice dissolving into a dark laugh. "Oh, oh, ohhh. *That's* why it's personal with her," he marveled aloud. "*That's* why she's been smirking at me since the moment I arrived."

Payne chuckled. "I take it when she was divulging the information she'd gleaned from your file she failed to mention that she'd actually applied for a job here?"

"Correct," he said, smiling, giving his head a shake. "She neglected to share that little tidbit."

"Well, I'm glad that I was able to enlighten you of that much, anyway."

"You wouldn't happen to have a copy of her résumé, would you?"

"I do, along with the background check that we ran on her after she came in."

Jay considered that. While his initial impulse was to ask for the additional file as well, ultimately…he did not. He didn't know why he was willing to offer her the privacy she hadn't afforded him, because, had she been a man, he had every certainty that he wouldn't have.

But she wasn't a man.

As he well knew.

And thank God, given his ridiculously insane pre-occupation with her. It was unnerving. Every sensation, feeling, inclination was heightened when it came to Charlie. He wasn't just intrigued with her—he was fascinated. He wasn't just attracted to her—he was drawn, compelled even. She didn't just annoy him—she infuriated him.

No doubt that was why he'd wigged out over her looking at his file, at her potentially reviewing the events leading up to his departure from the military.

Though he imagined that the gentlemen at Ranger Security were aware of the accident—and that he'd walked away unscathed—he, for reasons that escaped him, didn't want *her* to know about it.

It was too personal and his own feelings about what should have been a blessing were too convoluted in his own mind to consider discussing them with anyone else. One question would lead to another and eventually he'd wind up in territory he didn't want to explore.

"Just send me the résumé," Jay finally told Payne.

"You're sure?"

"I don't need her life story. I just need to know what she's capable of."

"Sometimes the two aren't mutually exclusive."

That was a good point, but it didn't change his mind. He merely chuckled. "She's definitely going to be a thorn in my side."

"And a perpetual pain in your ass until this is over," Payne said. Jay frowned. Was that a hint of admiration he heard in his boss's voice?

"What did you think of her?" Jay asked him, interested in his new boss's opinion of his newly acquired nemesis.

"I liked her," Payne said without preamble. "She's ballsy. She knew before she came in the door that we were going to turn her down, but she tried anyway. That takes guts."

So did hacking into their system, but he didn't think it prudent to remind Payne of that.

"You'll see her résumé. She's a former detective—a good one, based on reviews and recommendations—and, though she's small, she's a fighter. She teaches self-defense classes at several local colleges and battered women's shelters."

"Self-defense?"

"She's got a black belt in Tae Kwon Do," Payne explained. "Juan Carlos took one of her classes. He owed her a favor and brought her in for the interview."

Jay felt a line emerge between his brows. "Without your consent?"

An infinitesimal pause, but Jay caught it. "He was reprimanded."

Left in the dark again, Jay thought, renewed irritation spiking his blood pressure.

"I realize that I'm being purposely vague," Payne said, "but it's not my story to tell."

Ah. Well, at least that explained Juan Carlos's distinctly chilly welcome this morning. Had it only been this morning? Jay thought, disturbed. It already felt like a lifetime ago. For reasons that escaped him, he imagined that was Charlie Martin's fault. He knew a moment of bizarre premonition, knew beyond a shadow of a doubt that meeting her had marked a new era in his life, a before and after more significant even than his recent career change.

The thought jarred him, forcing him to dismiss it as melodramatic bullshit. Sheesh. He was losing his damned mind. He'd never been prone to any sort of bullshit, least of all the melodramatic variety.

It was *her,* Jay concluded. *She* was doing this to him.

"Why didn't you hire her?" he asked.

"Because you were better qualified."

And she wasn't a Ranger, Jay silently added. As far as he knew, the triumvirate—damn Juan Carlos for sticking that moniker in his head—hadn't hired anyone for field work other than former Rangers. In many ways he understood that. As Rangers themselves, McCann, Flanagan and Payne were aware of the training, the attention to detail, the skills and the mental agility required to get to that elite level of warrior status. Former Rangers were a known quantity with brotherhood-like bonds, ties that were formed on the battlefield, cemented with same experiences and, more often than not, baptized in some sort of blood.

Granted, Charlie Martin wasn't a former Ranger, but from what he could see, she would have brought an entirely different set of expertise to the Ranger Security staff. His lips quirked. No doubt her hacking skills would have come in handy. If she'd been made detective, then she'd worked her way up in the police force relatively quickly, seen the darker side of humanity. And, while she was small, those Tae Kwon Do skills meant that she knew how to protect herself.

That took discipline. He found himself reluctantly impressed.

As far as he could see, the only thing that had made him better qualified for the job was his military service, and, admittedly, that was by a narrow margin given her other skills. He knew his way around a computer well enough, but slinging code was a whole different skill set. It took a thoroughly organized—and in her case, slightly diabolical—mind.

And given the fact that they'd hired him instead of her, she was highly motivated to defeat him. A thrill of anticipation pushed adrenaline into his system, engaging his battle senses.

All right then, Kitty-Cat, Jay thought. *Game on.*

7

SMOKEY BURKHART HAD managed to live to the ripe old age of sixty-eight before falling in love.

He could honestly say he didn't much care for it.

He laid another log on the fire, then poked the coals around until the blaze stoked up again, licking the split timbers, curling around the bark. His Ms. Aggie enjoyed a fire. In fact, he didn't think he'd ever met another woman who liked one as much. She loved the scent of wood smoke, she'd once told him. Said it reminded her of her childhood in the Carolina hills.

Now it would forever remind him of her.

Over the years he'd heard love described in many different ways. He'd heard that it bloomed slowly, like a spring bud beneath the sun. That it had been instantaneous, a single inexplicable look and *bam!* Done. He'd heard about varying degrees of both, sometimes a combination of the two, but he'd never understood how a chance meeting or prolonged exposure to the same person could result in an affection that would render one essentially dependent on another for basic happiness.

He still couldn't explain it, but couldn't deny its existence anymore either.

She'd done that to him.

With a mere smile.

When he was feeling fanciful, which gallingly was happening more and more often, he imagined that the curve of her smile had hooked his heart and her laugh had literally reeled him in. By the time their initial interview was over he'd been leaning closer and closer to her, that was for damned sure, as though his body needed to be as near to hers as possible.

In truth, he hadn't required a job at all. He'd worked in forestry and conservation for the National Park Service for the better part of thirty years. The pay hadn't been anything to write home about, really, but the benefits were quite good and he'd invested well. It had been a job he'd enjoyed, one that had fulfilled him. He'd seen the absolute best the country had to offer, in parts that few others had ever been.

Though he probably could have stayed on another few years, he'd decided after a too-close call with a momma bear—one that had left him with a foot-long set of scars across his back and a shoulder that still ached—to leave it to the younger guys. To this day he still couldn't believe he'd missed her, that he'd made such a stupid, rookie mistake.

Water under the bridge.

He'd applied for this job purely out of boredom. A man could only tie so many fishing lures, and after a year of camping across the U.S. and another year putting the finishing touches on his cabin, he'd decided that he wasn't meant to be idle. Given the choice of greeting people at a local big-box store or being a well-dressed jack-of-all-trades at the Betterworth estate, he'd chosen the latter. He grunted under his breath.

As if he'd had a choice after meeting Ms. Aggie.

"Oh," the object of his torment breathed, pressing a hand to her chest. "I didn't realize you were still in here."

He hadn't meant to be. Typically, he tended her fire and then got the hell out of her room. The scent of her perfume hung in the air—honeysuckle and lavender (he'd checked)—and made him want to sniff the curve of her jaw, nuzzle the side of her neck. She was dressed for bed, a red chiffon gown that hung to her feet, the matching bed jacket across her shoulders. It was feminine and prim and proper—nothing remotely risqué—and yet the blood raced to his groin faster than a fox on a hare, and his mouth went bone-dry.

He stood slowly and dusted his hands. "I was just on my way out."

"It's rather late. You're welcome to stay here," she said, predictably. "Take one of the spare rooms."

She offered almost every night, but he always refused. Spending the night in the same house with her without spending the night *with* her was more torment than he could stand. It was bad enough being in the same house with her all day, every day, needing to be close to her, knowing it could never work out.

Smokey knew other men could probably get over the fact that a) she was his boss, and b) she had more money than he did, but Smokey wasn't one of those men. He knew that it was antiquated and old-fashioned…but what could he possibly offer a woman who could have whatever she wanted? What could he bring to the relationship that would have significant value? There wasn't anything in this world that he could give her that she couldn't get for herself. Sadly, the playing field was just too uneven—by several million dollars, in fact—and, at some point, he knew that would become an issue.

Better not to risk it.

The flip side to that coin? If he quit, he wouldn't get to see her at all. His gaze slid to her bare toes, which were curled adorably into the carpet. He snorted. Adorable? When did he start thinking in terms of adorable?

"I'd better not," he said, giving her a deferential nod. "I'll see you in the morning, Aggie."

He left while he still could.

But *damn* if it wasn't getting harder.

CHARLIE SQUASHED THE hint of regret that swelled in her traitorous heart, then quickly picked the lock securing Jay's door. It was unfortunate that a law-abiding citizen—one who in the past had sworn to uphold said law—had been reduced to such unorthodox tactics, but desperate times called for desperate measures.

She had to know what he'd slipped into his pocket earlier this afternoon. At this point, any clue was significant, and she couldn't afford not to be privy to whatever he'd found. The stakes were too high and failure simply wasn't an option.

She *had* to find the dog first.

That's what she'd kept telling herself this afternoon after he'd stormed away. Typically, when faced with the same sort of scenario, she could talk herself into believing that she'd done what she had to do. That winning in the boys' club meant not apologizing for being a hard-ass.

Unfortunately, for reasons she couldn't seem to figure out, the justification simply wouldn't come. It was that look, Charlie had ultimately decided. That fleeting flash of genuine fear that had flickered through his eyes. She hadn't been able to get it out of her head and, even worse, found herself genuinely concerned about what had put it there. What had he been afraid she'd find? What, exactly, haunted him?

Because clearly something did.

She'd been too preoccupied with alternately beating him and lusting after him to note the shadow lurking in that especially blue gaze, but once she'd paused long enough to really reflect, it was there.

Insanely, she wanted to fix it.

As if she could. As if that was her place. As if she hadn't gone stark-raving mad.

With a telltale click, the lock gave and she quietly slipped into the room. She'd patiently waited until she'd heard his shower start, then she'd sprung into action. She didn't know how long he'd be in the bathroom—her gaze darted in the direction of the en suite bath and she swore softly when she noted the open door—but she likely only had minutes to do what she needed to do.

A quick scan of the room revealed a tidy traveler, one who had stored his things in the empty closet and drawers and had set up his working area at the small desk in the corner of the room. She'd get to that, but in the meantime, where the hell were his pants? Not on the floor or slung carelessly over the back of a chair like a normal man, Charlie thought, growing increasingly nervous.

She picked up his cell phone and checked the last dialed call—Ranger Security. That didn't surprise her, and no doubt accounted for the smug smile he'd occasionally shot in her direction over dinner. They must have told him that she'd applied for the job and hadn't gotten it.

Renewed mortification stung her cheeks.

Oh well, Charlie thought with a bracing breath as she pulled up his email from his phone, she'd known he was going to find out. It had only been a matter of time. A message with an attachment from BPayne@RangerSecurity.com snagged her attention. The subject line said Charlie Martin's Résumé. Because she was shameless and couldn't resist, she opened the email.

As promised, here's the résumé. Let me know if you change your mind about looking over the background check. Sometimes knowing one's opponent is half the battle. —BP

Charlie felt her eyes widen and her face flame with anger—quite hypocritically, she would admit—at the invasion of her privacy. How dare they— Who in the hell did they think— A background check? On her? After they'd shown her the door? To what purpose?

She seethed.

Then stilled.

And read the message again.

Let him know if he changed his mind about seeing the background check? So Payne had offered and Jay had refused? Even knowing that she'd read every-thing she possibly could about him?

That was…unexpected. And undeservedly noble.

She exited the mail app and set the phone back down as though it had suddenly burst into flames.

Damn.

How was she supposed to fight dirty with a guy who was going to fight fair? This had never happened before. It was unprecedented, unfamiliar territory. She wasn't quite sure what to think, but a more press-ing matter arose and she pushed the conundrum to the back of her mind.

A mesh basket near the closet caught her attention. A collapsible hamper. Impressed—even she didn't travel with her own dirty-clothes hamper—she hur-ried over and snagged the pants out of the bottom, then pushed her hands into the pockets. She'd just felt something round and plastic brush her fingers when a noise from behind startled her.

Charlie reacted.

EVEN KNOWING THAT SHE had a black belt in Tae Kwon Do hadn't prepared Jay for how quickly she could strike. One second the sneaky, diabolical, opportunis-tic little wench had been prodding around in his pants pocket and the next she'd swung around and struck.

Gallingly, she'd connected with enough speed and force to send him toppling even though he'd had half a second to prepare. His legs flew out from under him and he landed flat on his back, with enough force to knock the breath from his lungs. Rather than check on him the way a normal, feeling woman would, she quickly whirled and grabbed his pants again, groping for the pocket.

Oh, hell, no.

Jay sprang up and tackled her from behind. Despite his bigger size, she managed to roll him with a well-placed elbow to the ribs. Pain shot through his middle and a stinging sensation ripped across his chest as he struggled to get the upper hand—hell, *any* hand.

"Get away from me," she grunted. "Or I'm really going to make you sorry."

He hadn't gotten enough breath back to talk to her, so instead he continued to try to subdue her. It was like trying to hold on to a damned tornado. She twisted and turned, struck out and clawed. Kitten, his ass, Jay thought—more like a feral cat. The only thing that kept her from landing another potentially brutal blow was the fact that he was literally on top of her more than he was off and she couldn't get enough strength behind her feet, legs or arms to really let him have it.

"I mean it, Jay. I'm giving you fair warning."

"Fair?" he managed to croak out, his eyes widening in mock astonishment. He dodged a knee to the groin, trapped her thigh. "That's rich. You've broken into my room, are going through my friggin' pants and you want to talk about fair?"

Her green-apple scent swirled around him and he was keenly aware of her soft breast against his chest. Damn, damn, damn. She was supple and strong and a strand of dark hair clung to her lush mouth and...

And typically, if he exerted this much energy with a woman it was for distinctly more pleasurable reasons.

But there was something quite thrilling about this, as well. He liked that she didn't give up, that she wasn't frightened or intimidated by him. He admired her skill, her courage, her sheer damned *nerve.*

Ballsy, Payne had said.

The thought had no more flitted through his head when she wrestled her small hand free and grabbed hold of his. He grunted with surprise and went utterly still, then looked down into her wide eyes.

He'd expected triumph—instead he saw shock.

That must have been when she realized he was naked.

He grinned.

She let go and shoved him away, then made for the door. *Oh, no. I don't think so.* Jay darted in front of her, blocking her path, and leaned casually against the door.

"What are you doing in my room?"

Color flying high on her cheeks, she looked at everything around her but him. "Put your towel back on," she said.

"You put it on me. You're the one who tore it off," he shot back, enjoying her discomfort much more than he would ever have believed. It was almost enough to make up for the fact that she'd Houdinied her way into his room. He spied his phone, noticed it was at a different angle from the way he'd left it. Irritation twisted through him, forcing him to pull a calming breath through his nose.

She was truly a piece of work.

"I didn't tear it off you," she said, shooting him an exasperated huff. "You snuck up on me," she accused. "What did you expect me to do?"

Seriously? That was her argument? His eyes widened significantly. "It's *my* room. One might argue that *you* snuck up on *me*." He crossed his arms over his chest. "What the hell are you doing in here?"

She pinched the bridge of her nose and closed her eyes tightly. Another deep sigh, then, "Could you please put your towel back on. That's…distracting."

"My room, my rules. I'll put the towel on when you tell me what you were doing…and what you found."

She emitted a low growl. "I was searching your things, obviously," she said, practically chewing the words between clenched teeth.

Her gaze darted to him once more, lingered over

his shoulders and chest, then she quickly looked away again. Impossibly, she blushed a deeper shade of red.

He grinned. "Yes, I'd rather worked that out for myself. What did you find?"

"Nothing of significance."

"You're lying," he said flatly. He was irrationally disappointed. Reason told him if she was unscrupulous enough to break into his room—hell, to hack into a prospective employer's system and then tell them about it—he shouldn't expect her to be honest, and yet... He hadn't pegged her for a liar.

Her gaze swung to his and he wondered what she'd heard in his voice because she swallowed hard and confessed. "Fine," she said. "I looked at your call log and checked your email."

He glanced at his computer. "Did you—"

"No," she said—then a droll smile rolled over her ripe lips. "I didn't have time."

He felt his own lips twitch at her candor. Maybe he hadn't pegged her too terribly wrong after all. Jay bent forward and grabbed the towel, then slowly—because she deserved it—anchored it once more around his hips. He heaved an exasperated sigh. "Honestly, woman, is there anything you won't do? Any line you aren't willing to cross?"

She blinked innocently. "I didn't download the attachment."

He snorted. "Because you already knew what was in it."

She jerked her chin toward his forgotten pants. "What's in the pocket?"

"If you were me, would you tell?"

"I told you about the peanut butter, didn't I?"

He leaned against the door once more and propped a foot against it. "That was an accident."

"What makes you say that?"

"The 'oh shit' expression immediately following the confession was a bit of a giveaway," he drawled. His gaze skimmed over her face, tracing the intriguing lines and angles, the plump mouth and wide eyes. "You have a very expressive face."

She blinked, seemingly startled.

He laughed softly and quirked a knowing brow.

She scowled and he laughed harder.

"Oh, to hell with it," she said, striding forward to leave. He'd rattled her enough to spark a retreat? Interesting.

"It was a bobber," he said.

She stopped short and looked up at him, her hand on the doorknob. "A bobber?"

"Yes. You know, to fish with."

Another line emerged between her finely arched brows and she bit into her bottom lip, evidently trying to make sense of what he'd just told her. "Is there a pond nearby? A lake? A creek?"

He shook his head. "Not on any map that I've looked at."

He was keenly aware of her—the slope of her

cheek, the angle of her jaw, the smooth creaminess of her throat. The sweep of her lashes, the absolute carnality of her mouth. His groin tightened and need shot through him, stark and fierce, with more intensity than he had ever experienced before. Her gaze tangled with his, then dropped to his mouth, lingered. Found his once more, and her pink tongue slid unconsciously along her full bottom lip.

He went hard.

Her breathing shallowed out and he watched her pulse flutter wildly at the base of her throat. Desire darkened her gaze, turned the green to emerald, the gold to bronze. He was hit with the almost overwhelming urge to slide his fingers along her cheek, to see if the skin was as soft and silky as it looked. To feel her sleek hair across the back of his hand, her ripe mouth beneath his. He didn't want just to taste her—he wanted to eat her up.

She drew a quick breath and dragged her gaze away from his. "Can I ask you something?" she said.

"You can ask. I reserve the right not to answer."

Something shifted in her expression. Hope, maybe? He frowned, trying to decipher what he saw.

"Why did you refuse the background check?"

Ah. He should have known that would pique her curiosity. "Because it doesn't have anything to do with what I came here for," he said.

"I would have deserved it," she told him, shooting him a chagrined look. "I wouldn't have blamed you."

He smiled down at her. "Yeah, but isn't it better that you don't have to?"

For once, her expression was completely unreadable. She returned his grin and nodded. Though he didn't really want her to leave—madness, with a bed that damned close—he pushed away from the door so that she could exit.

"Good night, Charlie," he murmured.

She darted another glance at him. Paused, seemingly uncertain, perplexed even. "Good night, Jay."

8

A SOFT, MUFFLED THUMP at his door awakened Jay from a halfhearted sleep. He quietly heaved himself up from the bed, grabbed a small flashlight and shrugged into his robe, then thrust his feet into his shoes.

Honestly, she was so damned predictable.

Jay had strung a thread of dental floss from the bottom of her door and attached it to a counterweight tube of toothpaste on the inside of his room, a few inches from his own door. When she opened her door, it pulled the floss tight enough on his end to slide the toothpaste forward, thus providing a thump loud enough to wake him but hopefully not her.

Sure enough, when he opened his door, hers had been left a fraction of an inch ajar, and a quick peek with his light confirmed an empty bed. She couldn't claim she needed to go to the bathroom because there was one in her room. It would be interesting to see what sort of story she'd provide when he found her.

Jay turned the flashlight off and, allowing his eyes to adjust to the dark, carefully made his way downstairs. He'd made his way through all of the lower rooms when he heard the telltale sound of a lock being thrown. And not just any lock. A dead-bolt. He felt his eyebrows wing up his forehead and swore hotly as his gaze shifted to the window. What the fu—

She was going outside?

It was bitter cold. If memory served—and it typically did—the low for tonight was five degrees. Jay headed to the front hall, where he found the alarm system had been disarmed and the door left partially open. He considered shutting it and waiting for her until she returned, letting her do a Little Match Girl impression before allowing her back into the welcoming warmth of the house.

Because he had to know what she was doing, he rejected that plan and made his way outside. He scanned the yard, looking for any sign of movement, and finally hit pay dirt when he glimpsed a flash of white near the gatehouse. Jay frowned, more intrigued than he'd like to admit. He'd talked to Burt, but other than the older man confirming the "probing" comment he'd made to Charlie and providing Jay with a pamphlet, as well, he hadn't pulled any sort of a vibe from him.

Evidently, Charlie had noticed something. Otherwise she wouldn't have braved this bone-chilling cold to search the little office unobserved.

Or so she thought.

Hiding behind the shrubbery, Jay covertly made his way toward the gatehouse. She'd already gotten inside—evidently her lock-picking skills were first-class, he thought drolly—and was bent over a drawer, aiming her own small flashlight into its depths. She read various bits of paper, occasionally frowned, swore and discarded them, then moved to the bottom cabinet of the built-in desk. Though he couldn't see what she'd found, if anything, it wasn't long until she straightened once more and turned to the fridge.

Nothing of note in the cabinet then, he concluded.

She pulled a soda from the fridge, selected a packet of cheese and crackers from Burt's stash, then sat down and fired up his computer. It was password protected, but she cracked it in a very admirable amount of time. He smiled despite himself.

Watching her work was genuinely fascinating. Her keen eyes scanned the contents of Burt's computer while her fingers flew across the keyboard. She paused occasionally to eat a cracker and sip her drink, frowning then smiling, and finally copied a few things to a little flash drive she'd produced from the pocket of her robe. She wore flannel sock-monkey pajamas, a fluffy white robe and sock-monkey slippers on her especially small feet. She looked completely in her element, confident and certain of her own abilities.

Her face was scrubbed bare, her button nose so clean it was shiny, and she'd pulled her hair up into a messy wad on top of her head. Frankly, there was nothing about her appearance that should elicit any sort of carnal response, and yet he found himself growing increasingly aroused.

He liked the way her mouth moved when she ate, the way her delicate throat muscles contracted when she swallowed. Her intriguing kittenish face held so much character it was hard to give it any of the traditional labels. *Pretty* simply didn't cut it, *beautiful* was too vague and *gorgeous* gave the wrong impression. Her lips were definitely the most sensual thing he'd ever laid eyes on, but even that didn't explain what it was about her that just did it for him. There was something about the way she cocked her head when she was thinking, the unmistakable intelligence in her large hazel eyes, the capable confidence with which she carried herself.

In a blinding moment of insight, he realized *that's* what made her different, *that's* what set her apart and tripped his trigger.

She was frighteningly smart, intimidatingly clever and more capable of taking care of herself than any woman he'd ever known. It was that utter assurance of her own ability that made her so singularly attractive.

He'd never met another woman like her. And he doubted he ever would.

She tilted her neck one way and then the other, then put her hands on the small of her back and gave a languorous stretch. Her unbound breasts pressed against her robe, making it gape open and he could see her pebbled nipples—for the first time in his life he was thankful for the cold—behind the soft fabric. She rolled her shoulders and yawned, then gave her head a little shake to jolt herself awake and set to work once more.

He watched her hack into Burt's email account, then his bank account, and finally check his browsing history. She played a word for him on his open Scrabble game—*observant,* for a double-word score—then updated his virus protection. Evidently confident that she'd found everything of note, she stuffed the cracker wrapper and empty drink bottle into her robe pocket and powered his computer down.

Observant, eh? He snorted. He'd see about that.

Jay waited for the light on the laptop to go off before scratching at the window. He watched her head jerk in his direction, her gaze narrow as she tried to see without any background illumination. After remaining motionless for a moment while she listened for further noise, she ultimately discounted the sound and continued tidying up.

He scratched again.

And this time when she looked in his direction, he put the flashlight under his chin and hit the light.

Predictably, she screamed.

LAUGHING SO HARD HE could barely breathe, Jay bent double in the little gatehouse and continued to mock her mercilessly.

"If you…could have…seen your face," he wheezed, his blue eyes streaming with tears of mirth. "Priceless," he chortled. "Classic," he wheezed. "Oh, God," he repeated hoarsely, over and over again. "That was— You *wailed*— And I—" Another exasperating fit of hilarity. "I don't know when I've ever heard that sort of noise out of a woman before in my life."

"It's all right," she said, waiting for her flaming face to cool. "Lots of men have trouble getting a woman to scream. There's probably a support group for that. You should ask Burt. I suspect he's a member."

He merely smiled wider, his blue eyes crinkling at the corners, an unexpected dimple in his right cheek. He ducked his head as though sharing a confidence. "Sweetheart, if the day ever comes that I can't make a woman scream, that's the day I'll eat my own hat."

Mercy. That smoldering look should have scorched all the hair off her face. She swallowed, suddenly unaccountably nervous. "You don't wear a hat."

He cocked his head and chuckled softly. "How do you know?"

She didn't, but... "You don't look like the hat type."

"There's a hat type?"

Feeling ridiculous and off-kilter, Charlie gave herself a shake. "Asinine prank aside, what the hell are you doing out here?"

"I followed you, obviously. The *asinine prank* was a belated stroke of genius." His shoulders shook with silent laughter again. They were broad, his shoulders, she noticed now. Well muscled and mouthwateringly wide.

She imagined licking one while she writhed naked beneath him, and a rush of warmth puddled in her core, making her squirm with want. Her traitorous nipples budded behind her pajama top, rasping against the soft fabric. She couldn't have been more shocked with herself than if she'd disrobed and pole-danced for him.

Of course, considering she'd grabbed him by the balls earlier this evening—felt his dick jerk against her hand and begin to swell—she should be past the point of shocking herself.

She also should have expected him to be watching her. Nevertheless, she'd thought she'd waited long enough for him to fall asleep. Her own eyes were drooping with fatigue now and she could feel the day's events catching up with her. She wasn't at her sharpest when she was tired and didn't have the mental ability to keep up with him right now, much less stay a step ahead.

He searched her face and he sobered a bit, his expression becoming one of affectionate concern. "Tired, Kitty-Cat?"

She didn't know what was more disturbing—the expression or the nickname. "Kitty-Cat? Oh, right," she said. "I clawed you. Earlier," she qualified at his bemused expression.

"What?"

"In your room," she told him. "When you startled me, remember?"

He continued to stare blankly at her.

"Oh, for heaven's sake," she said, reaching forward to open his robe. Her finger lightly traced an angry line on his chest and they winced simultaneously— her in regret, him in pain.

He looked down, as though just seeing the reddened skin for the first time and blinked. "Damn. So you did."

"You hadn't noticed?"

He continued to look at her finger against his chest and the air between them suddenly shifted, grew heavier and warm. Golden curly hair clung to his impressive pecs and bisected his abdomen in a darker line that disappeared beneath the elastic band of his boxers. His abs were rock hard and well formed, the traditional coveted six-pack. His nipples were dusky

dark and slightly puckered. She noticed a half-moon–
shaped scar beneath one and had to forcibly keep herself from touching it as well, as though his body were
hers to explore, his various scars, freckles and moles
a treasure map of masculine sexuality.

He released a shuddering breath and she felt his
hand tentatively cup her cheek, his thumb lightly
trace the curve of her jaw. His fingers were gratifyingly unsteady—hesitant even—and that single hint
of uncertainty, the idea that she might not welcome
his touch, was what ultimately made her look up.

He was staring at her cheek, where his hand met it,
specifically, and the look on his face made her heart
squeeze with some new emotion she didn't recognize
because she'd never felt it before. It was bittersweet
and triumphant and *wonderful*.

His gaze met hers then, desire a blue flame lighting them from within, and, though only a second ago
he might have been cautious, the kiss he suddenly
pressed against her lips was not. It was thrillingly
sure, bone-meltingly competent and had the magical
ability to burn through her body like wildfire, singeing nerve endings, charring any good sense and res-
ervations and leaving her all but utterly liquefied.

She sighed against his talented lips, leaned into
him and slid her hands up and over his chest, along
his shoulder and neck, then into his hair. He groaned
against her mouth and deepened the kiss, tangling his
tongue around hers. Heat swept her up in a tornado of

sensation and she leaned farther into him. He settled against the edge of the desk, widened his legs into a deeper V so that she could fit between them and drew her closer. His warm fingers explored her jaw and slid into the hair at the nape of her neck, making gooseflesh race across her scalp, while his other hand molded around her waist. She felt strangely safe and protected beneath his touch, feminine but not fragile.

She shivered from the inside out, her breasts plumped and tingled and the skin between her legs dampened and throbbed, ripening for him. He dragged his lips along her cheek, his nose along her jaw and inhaled, breathing her in, before bringing his lips back to her mouth. She could feel the tension in his body, the desire blistering through his skin, the sinfully hot ridge of his arousal nudging against her belly.

She swallowed a whimper, left his mouth and licked a path along the slightly salty side of his neck, then nipped at his earlobe. Gratifyingly, he shivered and drew her closer, lifting her up until she could feel him nestled at the top of her thighs.

Oh, sweet hell, Charlie thought as he sucked her tongue into his mouth. His big hands shaped her bottom and squeezed, managing to align her so perfectly that when she so much as breathed, pleasure bloomed in her sex.

She was a few inhalations away from a *spectacular* orgasm.

And as much as she'd love that…she couldn't let it happen.

With a sigh of regret, she broke free and stepped back.

He blinked at her for a moment, then sanity returned to his gaze and he passed a hand over his face.

"Sorry," he said. "I—"

"No, it's fine," she told him, because the last damned thing she wanted him to be was sorry that he'd kissed her. She was lots of things at the moment—hot, bothered and unsatisfied, for starters—but her only regret was not being able to take this to its natural conclusion.

But she couldn't. Not with him. He was The Enemy, she reminded herself with a bracing breath. The guy who'd taken her dream job. The guy she was bound and determined to best. Looking to him for a little mutually satisfying sex would be the height of stupidity, and while Charlie would admit to some occasional dumbass-ness, she was rarely unforgivably stupid.

And sleeping with Jay Weatherford would certainly be that.

He straightened and pushed away from the edge of the desk. "You know what?" he said matter-of-factly. "I lied."

"What?"

"I lied," he repeated. "I'm not sorry. I apologized because it felt like the right thing to do, but I'm not sorry. I've been thinking about kissing you all day—" his broody gaze dropped to her mouth, making her lips tingle anew "—and I'm not sorry that I did it because it only confirms what I expected all along."

Charlie couldn't quite catch her breath. "Oh? What was that?"

"That you have the best mouth I've ever seen," he said baldly. "It's unbelievably hot. Soft, plump, ripe and better-tasting than any other." He waited for her to say something, but she couldn't. She was too stunned to speak. "Now's when you're supposed to pay me a compliment, too," he said, gesturing magnanimously. "Doesn't have to be as eloquent as mine, but it's only good manners to repay it in kind."

Charlie struggled to form a coherent thought. She'd never met a guy quite like Jay, one who was so forthright and honest. "You…"

He smiled encouragingly. "Yes?"

"You… You have nice shoulders," she blurted out.

His face went comically still. "That's a new one on me, but I'll take what I can get." He paused. "And I mean that literally. Fair warning, Charlie. I'm going to kiss you again."

Panic punched her heart rate into a swifter rhythm. "Oh, no. I—" More kissing would inevitably lead to more…of everything else.

"I know it's a bad idea," he said, reading her mind. He shrugged helplessly. "We're opponents working for rival companies. I've got the job you wanted. You want to annihilate me. I get it. But—" He stepped forward again, lessening the distance between them, and slid his thumb across her bottom lip. His lids dropped to half-mast and he sighed softly, then brushed her mouth once more with his. "—I know my own strength and this is a battle I'm not going to win."

She lifted her chin. "Just because you can't win your battle doesn't mean I can't win mine," she said, striving for some sort of mental high ground.

He grinned at her. "True," he said. "But you've got to want to win it…and you don't want to any more than I do."

And the hell of it was…she knew he was right.

Damn.

9

"THERE'S BEEN A DEVELOPMENT," Aggie said when Charlie and Jay practically skidded into the room. Jay was gentleman enough to let her enter first, a gesture of courtesy too many women these days didn't appreciate.

While Aggie was well aware that women had earned their spots in the work force, she'd never understood the I'll-get-my-own-door mentality some of them subscribed to. Opening a door, pulling out a chair, standing when a woman rose from the table. These were things her parents had taught their sons, lessons she'd passed on to her boys.

Evidently Jay's mother and father had taken the time to teach him, as well. It was heartening to see that, to know that some people still remembered and appreciated old-school deportment.

He nodded in her direction. "Good morning, Ms. Aggie."

She smiled at him. "Morning, dear. I trust you slept well."

He flashed a grin. Goodness, what a handsome devil. "Like a baby, thank you."

The telltale smudges beneath Charlie's eyes told her that the younger woman hadn't fared as well, but she asked all the same. "And you, Charlie?"

Her gaze darted fleetingly to Jay, then a smile that was just a little wan and too hesitant shaped her lips. "Fine, ma'am. You said there was a development. What's happened?"

Aggie released a nervous breath. "The ransom instructions were delivered sometime during the night. Smokey found them this morning when he arrived."

Jay's gaze sharpened. "Found them where?"

"On the gatehouse. They were taped to the window."

For whatever reason, that made Charlie blush. "Burt didn't find them?"

"No," Aggie said. "Burt arrives at seven." She hesitated. "Smokey typically gets here a little earlier."

Because Aggie was an early riser and liked to prepare her own breakfast, it had become their habit to share the meal together without Jasmine or any of the other staff. She absolutely cherished that time. It was her favorite part of the day, watching him duck into the kitchen, then smile when he saw her, the light reaching his wise eyes.

"What time did he get here this morning?" Jay asked.

"Five-thirty." He liked to watch her cook, had said seeing a woman move around the kitchen was the second-best way to start a morning. She'd never mustered the courage to ask what he thought the *best* way to start the morning was. She expected his answer would make her blush.

"Could we see it?" Jay asked.

Aggie noted the *we* with pleasure. A quick glance at Charlie confirmed that she'd caught the use of the plural, as well. She looked almost startled, for lack of a better description. As though she wasn't used to a man who wasn't trying to put his own interests first.

"Of course." Aggie retreated to the library table to retrieve the missive and then handed it to Charlie. She'd hired her, after all. It only seemed right. Furthermore, she wanted to see what Charlie would do, to see if she'd willingly share the information that had just been put into her hands.

"I wish I had some gloves," Charlie muttered as she carefully withdrew the note. "I feel like I'm destroying whatever evidence might be here."

"The last letter was clean," he told her. "No prints, no trace." He nodded toward the pasted-letter note. "No doubt this one is, as well."

Charlie made a moue of concession and studied the instructions. A line knitted her brow.

"What is it?" Aggie wanted to know.

"Something about this is nagging me," she said. "I feel like I should be recognizing something here."

The same expression was written across Jay's face. "I'm pulling the same vibe. I can't put my finger on it, but…"

She looked up at him. "I know. I feel like I've seen it before—and I have, in the other letter, of course—but this is different."

They bent their heads over the note, scrutinizing it further. "They want the money wired into an off-shore account," Jay said. "That's clean. It doesn't give us any chance at all of meeting them. Catching them. Finding anything incriminating."

"And look at this," Charlie pointed out. "They're going to text the account number to Aggie's phone in scrambled intervals—my guess, with several disposable cell phones—with a sixty-second window to make the transfer." She looked up at him. "That's slick. It doesn't leave any time to investigate the account. Chances are they're going to be ready to immediately move the money again—sweep it directly into another account—and close the original."

"Should we go that route?" he asked. "Would you have enough time to hack into the system?"

She winced thoughtfully. "I don't know. Sixty seconds isn't a long time. And definitely not with the equipment I brought with me."

"I don't understand half of what you just said, but I can get you whatever you need," Aggie interjected.

"Obviously, I'll pay the ransom." Her voice broke, but she collected herself when they both looked up at her. "But I will not release one red cent until I know for sure that my Truffles is fine, that not a hair on her little body has been harmed."

"It says here that they will text the location of the dog once the transfer is complete."

Aggie's lips formed a hard smile. "Then I guess this is what one would call a Mexican standoff, because I won't transfer the money without confirmation that my dog is alive and well."

Charlie winced. "Until we find them, we have no way of communicating that."

"In the event that we don't apprehend them before the first set of numbers arrives, we'll simply have to text back," Jay said.

"We can't if they block the number," Charlie pointed out.

"Surely you can find your way around that." There was admiration in his tone.

Aggie watched a smile bloom over Charlie's lips, observed Jay's sudden preoccupation with her mouth, then saw Charlie's cheeks pinken in response.

Well, well, well. It was entirely possible the two of them were going to do more than learn to work together. Imagine that. Her, an inadvertent matchmaker. How lovely.

Charlie tucked a stray strand of hair behind her ear and turned to look at Aggie. "It's my sincere hope that you don't have to pay the ransom, Ms. Aggie, and with that in mind, I'd like to ask you a few more questions."

"Of course, dear. I'll help in any way I can."

"Was there any particular reason that Burt didn't receive a gift from Goldie upon her death? He told me that he'd worked for the estate for twenty years. You mentioned that other faithful employees had been generously rewarded for their service and I just wondered…" She trailed off.

Aggie smiled. "You want to know why Goldie didn't leave Burt any money?"

Charlie shrugged helplessly. "Well…yes, actually."

"If you've talked to Burt, then you know the answer to that already. Goldie knew that if she left Burt money he'd funnel it all into that UFO club of his. Instead, she bought Burt a house and gave it to him with the stipulation that it can never be mortgaged except in the event of extenuating circumstances. Illness and the like," she told them. "Burt cashed out his retirement the year before Goldie died and made a documentary about people who had been 'probed' by aliens." She gave a delicate shudder. "Blew the whole thing on fancy cameras and editing equipment and spent thousands of dollars traveling across the country to interview other probees. Years of savings gone in a matter of months." She winced. "Goldie was heartbroken. She didn't want him to end up with nowhere to live, so making sure he had a home was her first priority."

Charlie inclined her head knowingly. "Ah." She chewed the inside of her cheek. "He neglected to mention that part."

"He doesn't think about it," Aggie told her. "He mans the gate, chats with other UFO enthusiasts online and plays Scrabble. He's…different," she added, trying to find a word that would adequately describe the odd gatekeeper. "But harmless."

"Would you like some tea, ma'am?" Jasmine asked from the doorway.

"Yes, please, Jasmine," Aggie told her. "That would be lovely."

"How long has she worked for you?" Jay wanted to know, shooting a speculative look after the cook.

"About ten months," Aggie told him. "I have trouble keeping a cook." She laughed softly. "Evidently I don't eat enough to justify having one, but—" she shrugged "—it's a treat for me. Years of putting dinner on the table for other people, worrying over what everyone liked, should I have made something different—that will do it to you."

"Perfectly understandable," Charlie said, smiling at her. "I'd love to have a cook."

Seemingly surprised, Jay looked over at her. "You can't cook?"

"Of course I can," she said with an exasperated

eye roll. "I just don't like cooking for one. It doesn't taste as good."

"That doesn't make any sense."

She glared up at him. "Can you cook?"

"I can grill," he said. "And microwave."

She gave her head a small shake. "Why are we talking about this?"

That's what Aggie would have liked to know. But it was vastly entertaining. If she weren't so concerned about the safe return of her pet she'd be delighted for them to continue. As it was, she needed them to focus.

"Do either of you have any more questions for me?" she asked kindly.

Their startled expressions swiveled toward her as though they'd both forgotten she was there.

"I found a fishing bobber on the other side of the fence," Jay remarked. "It's probably nothing, but I wondered if there were any ponds nearby."

Aggie frowned, pondering the question, then shook her head. "The Whitmoors have an elaborate goldfish pond, but that's purely decorative."

He pulled a face. "I thought as much, but still wanted to ask."

"Does Truffles like peanut butter?" Charlie wanted to know.

Aggie grinned, her heart aching for her pet. "She *adores* it. She's got a toy that I fill with peanut butter and freeze. She'll spend hours licking the peanut butter out of it."

Jay and Charlie shared a look.

"What?" Aggie asked, trepidation tightening her belly.

"We think Truffles was baited," Charlie said. "I found a smear of peanut butter on the back wall."

Aggie felt a frown knit her brow. "Baited? But how did they get her out of the yard?"

Jay shrugged and exhaled a long breath. "That's the million-dollar question. But when we find the answer we'll have our culprit."

"Speaking of which," Charlie said significantly. "I'd better get started."

So she was back to *I,* was she? Aggie noted, mildly disappointed. "If you'll make a list of that computer equipment you need, I'll send Smokey out to get it for you."

"Thanks," Charlie said gratefully. "That would be a big help."

Aggie nodded. "Consider it done."

She watched Jay go in one direction and Charlie go in another. Sadly, it reminded her of another man and woman who couldn't seem to get on the same path.

And she was tired of walking alone.

IT WOULD HAVE BEEN HELPFUL to know that Burt had been working at the Betterworth estate for the past twenty years and hadn't been given any cash as the other employees had, Jay thought, irrationally irritated that a) Charlie hadn't told him about it, b) that he'd asked her last night and had gotten so damned distracted from his line of questioning by that incendiary kiss that he'd completely forgotten to press the issue and c) that he had neglected to ask the right question in the first place.

Ultimately, it was no one's fault but his own, but knowing that didn't make him feel any better. Had she kissed him because she hadn't wanted to answer his questions? Because she'd needed to distract him and she'd used his own desire against him? Hadn't that been *his* original plan?

How galling.

Even more degrading? He'd do it all over again… and fully intended to. That kiss… His gut constricted with remembered desire, his groin tightened and a low breath leaked out of his lungs. While Jay had never been what one would call a player, he'd nevertheless spent a good bit of time honing his skills in the bedroom. He knew when to kiss, when to suck, when to caress, when to nuzzle and when to take things to the next level.

Because he was competitive, he wanted to be the best, so he'd also made it a point to be a selfless lover. A slow smile slid over his lips. Meaning he wouldn't *scream* until she did.

And right now, he wanted nothing more than to make her scream until she couldn't breathe, until she was hoarse from the effort, until the same little claws that had torn into his chest when they'd rolled around on the floor last night were scoring his back.

He wanted her with a ferocity that was unparalleled, unmatched and wholly unexpected. When his mouth had touched hers, the rest of the world had simply retreated out of existence. The feel of those unbelievably carnal lips beneath his—the ripe taste of her—had simply undone him.

Jay wasn't used to coming undone. In fact, he was typically the one doing the undoing, so even admitting that she'd affected him as thoroughly as she had instilled a tiny drop of panic into his chest.

There was something different about her, he realized. Something beautiful and sweet, strong, witty and endearing. When he looked at her, he felt as if his feet were flying out from under him. His lips twitched. Much like last night when she'd literally cut him off at the knees and sent him sprawling onto the carpet. That took some serious skill, and when he considered that she'd done it—his petite little warrior—he was unreasonably proud of her.

How ignorant was that?

Evidently she'd knocked him senseless when she'd felled him, Jay thought.

And the idea that she'd played him, that she might not be as intrigued and lit up as he was…

Jay growled under his breath and made himself focus on the task at hand. Irritatingly, he'd gotten a summons this morning to Andrew Betterworth's townhouse on the French Broad River and was reluctantly making his way there now. Honestly, it felt like a monumental waste of time. He'd been regularly emailing Andrew with updates, but coming over here was stupid and drew him away from time better spent in pursuit of the dognappers.

That was what Charlie was doing, he thought, annoyed all over again. Who knew what sort of clues she was going to find while he wasn't watching her? What sort of advantage she'd garner?

He located the right house number, noting the fancy sports car in the driveway. It was red with black racing stripes and the vanity plate read Eat It.

Nice.

He hadn't met Andrew yet and already hated him. Determined to get this over with as quickly as possible, Jay made his way to the door and knocked.

A curvy blonde with a black eye answered the door. She kept her head turned to limit his view and pulled a hank of hair over the offending bruise.

Jay's blood boiled and he felt his fingers tighten.

"Is that him?" an obnoxious male voice shouted from somewhere deep in the house. "Bitch, I'm talking to you! Is that him?"

The woman flinched and shot him an apologetic look. Upon closer inspection she couldn't have been more than twenty, if that. "Are you Jay Weatherford?"

"I am."

"It is," she called over her shoulder.

"Then let the man in the door, dumbass," he sneered. "And get us something to drink."

By the time Jay had crossed the threshold he was ready to pummel the hell out of his so-called employer. Though he knew he'd been this mad before, he didn't think he'd ever felt so dangerous, so on the verge of making a critical tactical error.

The house looked as though it had been decorated by a pimp who only recognized animal prints. Jay had never seen so much zebra in his life. Dozens of candles littered the room, all of them burning with different scents, and a fire blazed on the hearth.

"Ah," Andrew Betterworth drawled as Jay came into view, tearing his gaze away from the flames. "My own personal badass. You're late."

If Andrew seriously thought he was going to be able to intimidate him, he had another think coming. Jay nonchalantly checked his watch. "No, I'm not. I'm two minutes early. And this is a waste of my time."

Evidently unaccustomed to anyone daring to defy him, Andrew looked him over and smirked. "Since I'm the one paying for it, it's my place to say what is or what isn't a waste of your time, isn't it?"

"You're paying me to do a job and preventing me from doing it. That's stupid," Jay said baldly. He pulled a lazy shrug and dropped into a chair without being asked. "But when you're dumb you've got to be tough. And in your case, poor to boot. I'm here. What did you want?"

"A more respectful attitude would be a good start."

"I don't respect bullies," Jay said through clenched teeth as the young blonde came back into the room. "And my respect isn't for sale."

Her legs were bruised as well, he noted, particularly the insides of her thighs. Bile rose in his throat. *Jesus.* She set a tray of drinks on the coffee table, but Andrew snagged her arm before she could go and dragged her down into his lap. "Stay," he said, as though commanding a dog.

She looked terrified, mortified and utterly cowed.

"I'd like a status update on the case," Andrew said, leveling a look at Jay while he casually—sickeningly—stroked the girl's arm.

"I emailed that to you this morning. The ransom instructions arrived earlier." Much as he hated to do it, he explained the terms.

"It sounds quite foolproof."

"Well, it's not, Andrew," Jay told him, seriously ashamed that this was the man he was working for. Aggie had been right. There was no concern for the animal his aunt had loved, nothing but greed and a nasty, soulless temperament.

Andrew squeezed his eyes tightly shut and when he looked up he was angrily exasperated. The girl didn't so much as move a muscle, had gone as still as a rabbit who had picked up the scent of a wolf.

"It's *On*-drew. *On*-drew! Why can't any of you inbred hicks get it right?"

Jay blinked. "I'm sorry?"

His client heaved a long-suffering sigh, as though this were an explanation he'd grown weary of making. "My name is pronounced *On*-drew. Not Andrew." He said it slowly, as though he were instructing a half-wit.

Jay felt his lips twitch. It was just too damned ridiculous. Too pretentious. "Right. Got it."

Ondrew's thin nostrils flared with irritation. "You think this is funny? That my name is a joke?"

"Not at all." He smothered another laugh.

Evidently, that was the last straw. Andrew bolted up from the chair, dumping the blonde onto the floor in the process.

"Hey!" Jay shouted. "What the hell are you doing?"

Andrew gave her a hard kick in the ribs. "Get out of my way, you stupid cow," he growled, trying to go around her.

Jay saw red. Literally.

Before he knew what he was doing, he'd laid Andrew out flat, blood pouring from his undoubtedly broken nose.

The girl screamed while Andrew's nasal profanities filled the air. Jay looked at the blonde. "Do you want to stay here?"

She gave her head an emphatic shake. "No."

"Bitch, you'd better not leave me!" Andrew spat. "I'm warning you. You leave and you can forget your modeling career. No more photo shoots! No more designer labels!"

Showing the first bit of spunk, the girl drew her foot back and kicked him right in the groin. He grunted, wheezed and his face turned purple. "I lied," she said. "It *is* little."

Andrew glared daggers at Jay. "You'll pay for this," he said brokenly.

"Ask me if I care, *An*drew." He looked at the girl. "What's your name?"

"Josie."

He jerked his head toward the door. "Let's go."

The minute he got in the car he dialed Ranger Security and asked for Payne. "We've got a problem," he said grimly.

"What?"

Jay shifted into Drive and aimed the car toward the Betterworth estate. "I just decked Andrew Betterworth and left with his girlfriend. Be on standby to make my bail."

10

BECAUSE THE LETTERING on the newest note seemed so
familiar, Charlie had made a copy and kept reviewing it. Presently, she'd returned to the house after a
futile search for additional clues around the perimeter of the estate.

Predictably, she'd found nothing.

It was as though Truffles had vanished into thin
air. She rolled her eyes. As though he'd been plucked
from the sky by one of Burt's UFOs. Something nig-
gled in the back of her mind, a fleeting realization
that would never fully form, then retreated annoyingly to the ether.

"Are you sure I can't make you anything else?"
Jasmine wanted to know.

The girl was thin and dark, with large almond-
shaped eyes and multiple piercings in her ears, nose
and eyebrows. Hat tip to Ms. Aggie for hiring her,
Charlie thought. Typically, Jasmine was the sort of

girl that wealthy people wouldn't want around. She didn't look dangerous, but she did look different and that, oftentimes, would be enough to make her an outcast.

"No, thanks," Charlie told her. "The panini was wonderful. Where did you learn to cook like that?"

"I used to work at the Rose and Dove out on the French Broad. We made lots of specialty sandwiches and salads. I enjoyed it. Pairing unexpected flavors and such." She wiped down the kitchen counters. "Ms. Aggie isn't much of an eater, really. She makes her own breakfast—" she shot Charlie a covert smile over her shoulder "—for her and Mr. Smokey, but she doesn't know that I know that, so don't mention it."

Charlie grinned. Ms. Aggie and Smokey? Seriously. Wow. She paused, allowing the couple to gel in her mind, and realized that they matched. Ms. Aggie was open and warm and Smokey seemed wise and reserved. "How do you know that?"

"She leaves the dishes in the sink," Jasmine told her. "At first I thought she was inviting Burt in and feeding him—" a fleeting scowl raced across her face "—but when I asked him about it, Burt didn't know what I was talking about."

Charlie had noticed that Jasmine seemed to have a soft spot for the eccentric Burt. She'd put extra helpings on his plate at lunch and had made him an Oreo cupcake for his dessert. For whatever reason, Charlie's spidey senses were tingling. "Burt's quite a character," she said.

"He reminds me of my father," Jasmine remarked thoughtfully, staring out the window. She had a perfect uninterrupted view of the backyard, Charlie realized.

"Oh? How so?"

She sighed. "Like Burt, he was passionate about something people didn't understand."

"Then he must have been a very courageous man. It takes guts to be passionate about things other people ridicule."

Jasmine turned then, her expression one of delighted surprise. "That's true," she said wonderingly. "I'd never thought of it that way before." She nodded, a soft smile on her lips. "He was courageous. And he was a good man. Undervalued, but good."

Undervalued? Like Burt? Or was it because Burt was into UFOs? "I'm sorry for your loss."

"It's been a long time," she said. "He died when I was fifteen."

That was certainly an impressionable age. Charlie was dying to know what Jasmine's father had been so passionate about, but since the girl hadn't shared that information, she didn't see how she could ask without being callous or prying.

A chime sounded, indicating a car was coming up the driveway, and Charlie's heart gave a little kick of hopefulness at the idea that it could be Jay. He'd left

earlier this morning—none too happily—to go and
see Andrew Betterworth.

She didn't understand why his client would want
him to take time away from the case. Though she'd
appreciated the time to do a little poking around without him looking over her shoulder, inexplicably...
she'd missed him.

Not good.

How in the world could she possibly miss someone she'd just met? How could she care about where
he was or what he was doing when, beyond this case,
he wasn't going to be part of her life? He was The
Enemy. Her nemesis. The bane of her recent existence. And yet...

She wanted him to make her *scream.*

Loudly.

A shudder of need shivered over her shoulders
at the thought, and she resisted the urge to bite her
fist as desire wended its way through her once more.
Just thinking about him—about his lips against hers,
his mouth on her neck, his hands on her ass—made
something hot and achy slither through her.

Furthermore, he was every bit as crafty as she was.
The dental-floss-tied-to-the-toothpaste trick had been
friggin' ingenious. She wished she'd thought of it and
had been trying to come up with ways to replicate the
alarm herself. No doubt he'd be doing his own snoop-
ing around the house tonight, just to prove to her that
he could.

Another night with no sleep.

But that wasn't what was important. Getting the dog back was the main goal here. And thankfully, that goal coincided with beating Jay, so she was all good on that score. For the first time in her life, she wished that she could be different, that she could look at this assignment without seeing it as a competition...but she couldn't.

She knew that Jay Weatherford was a kick-ass soldier and that he was undoubtedly just as qualified for the job at Ranger Security as she'd been. But she genuinely believed that she brought a different skill set to the team that should have put her a hairbreadth ahead of him. For whatever reason, she suspected that her hacking skills were going to be the key to unraveling who had taken Ms. Aggie's dear dog.

She wouldn't claim that she was always going to be the better agent. But in this case, she thought she was. Arrogant? No doubt that's what a man would say. But she liked to call it "honest."

Furthermore, much as she hated to admit what she was contemplating—particularly considering the grace he'd shown her—the idea of hacking into the military files to take a peek at Jay's history was becoming more and more appealing. Should she do it? No. But intuition told her that whatever had put that flash of fear in his eyes could be found in those files. And she wanted to know what had caused it.

Kitty-Cat, he'd called her. Her lips twisted. Apropos, considering it was her curiosity that got her into trouble the majority of the time.

The door opened then and Charlie turned, curing the smile that had jumped instantly to her lips. It was Jay, of course. He had blood on his knuckles and shirt, and the girl with him was sporting a day-old black eye and bruises in various degrees of healing. She looked relieved, but frightened. Charlie had spent enough time in shelters to know what a battered woman looked like.

The question was, where the hell had Jay found her?

Charlie sprang up from her chair, offered a welcoming smile and extended her hand. "I'm Charlie," she said. "It's nice to meet you."

The young woman looked at Jay for guidance, and at his nod, she offered a tentative smile. "I'm Josie," she said. "Josie Miller."

A muscle flexed in Jay's jaw. "Josie is Andrew Betterworth's former girlfriend. The blood on my shirt belongs to him. I'm certain I'm fired and almost as sure that I'll be going to jail soon."

Charlie couldn't have been any more shocked if he'd announced that he'd given up personal security to be a ballet dancer. A thought struck and she inhaled sharply. "You didn't—" She swallowed. "You didn't kill him, did you?"

Jay and Josie both blinked, then glanced at each other and started laughing. "No," Jay told her. "I didn't kill him. But his nose and his nuts are in bad shape. The nose is my fault." He jerked his head in Josie's direction, seemingly proud of her. "She's responsible for the nut injury."

The admiration in his tone made Josie stand a little straighter. "He deserved it," she said with a succinct nod.

Looking at all the abuse he'd heaped on this poor girl, Charlie imagined he deserved anything Jay and Josie had given him and more. *Bastard.*

"Did you kick him with the heel of your foot?" Charlie asked.

"Yes."

She cocked her head. "Barefoot or with a shoe?"

"Barefoot."

"Good. It'll hurt longer." Strictly speaking, Charlie didn't know if this was true or not, but the pleasure that animated Josie's battered face was worth the potential lie.

In her experience, women who had been abused typically wanted a bath—to wash their abuser away—and a soft, safe place to land for a while. She wasn't sure what Ms. Aggie would say about taking in the young woman for a few days, but Charlie could certainly provide her with the temporary use of her en-suite bath and a few clothes until decisions were made about her future.

"Why don't you come with me?" Charlie said. "And I'll get you settled."

By the time Josie was bathed, newly clothed and moved into her own room, the police had arrived and taken Jay into custody.

Andrew had pressed charges.

With any luck, he would get his own time behind bars, because Charlie was going to encourage Josie to press charges, as well. She'd been systematically mentally and physically abused. She was eighteen. A runaway whom Andrew had "saved," dangling the idea of a modeling career in front of her. Josie wasn't stupid—she was just a product of her circumstances. A drug-addict mother, a perverted stepfather. She'd fled at seventeen.

Charlie had heard it so many times before. Too many.

Even though she knew that Ranger Security was more than likely going to make a phone call and get Jay out of jail, Charlie nonetheless went down to see him. Predictably, bond had been set and paid and, when he walked out, he looked endearingly tired, unbelievably sexy and heart-stoppingly gorgeous.

He smiled when he saw her, his blue eyes crinkling at the corners. Her chest tightened to the point where she couldn't breathe, and she grew lightheaded. She could feel her pulse thundering in her ears, the steady *galug-galug-galug* telling her something she didn't want to hear, didn't want to acknowledge.

This man had cold-cocked an abuser, rescued the abused women and forfeited his job in the process.

Would Ranger Security fire him? Certainly not. No doubt any one of them would have done the same thing when faced with the same dilemma. But he'd undoubtedly cost them a lot of money, a potential lawsuit and a headache of massive proportions. She was so full of emotion—pride and gratitude and happiness, of all things—she feared she'd burst.

And he hadn't cared.

He smiled down at her, his gaze warm and surprised. "I could have called a cab, Kitty-Cat. What are you doing here?"

Charlie grabbed his shirt by the lapels and drew him down to her. She slid her nose along one side of his, nuzzling, breathing him in. "Giving you a hero's welcome," she murmured, before pressing her lips to his.

_11_

"IF YOU'RE GOING TO do this every time I hit someone, then the general population isn't safe," Jay told her, chuckling against her mouth. Like a match to dry tinder, need flamed inside him, singeing his veins, making his scalp prickle, his dick swell.

Catcalls, whoops and whistles eddied around them, reverberating off the cinder-block walls, but he couldn't seem to care. As a rule, he'd never been much of a fan of PDAs, but he'd never been kissed like this before, and frankly, much like Rhett Butler, he simply didn't give a damn.

In fact, he imagined that any time at all around Charlie Martin would make him permanently indifferent to everyone but her. If he'd had the presence of mind to sincerely consider that thought, no doubt it might have given him pause.

But his mind didn't play in any part of this, other than to process feeling and sensation, to send the signals to his brain that would command his muscles to bring her closer to him.

He needed to be closer. As close as he could possibly get.

Beneath her skin, the way she'd gotten under his.

She was hot and warm and soft and he could feel the desire shimmering off her and curling around his own and it was nothing short of magical the way she felt against him. Her skin was silky to the touch, her body curvy but firm and well honed, her fingers strong and insistent as they roamed over his face, his neck and along his shoulders. She mewled and purred in his mouth and he ate those sounds, savored them against his tongue.

Holy hell, how he wanted her.

An especially loud "ahem" sounded from directly behind him and they reluctantly drew apart. Jay sent a sheepish look over his shoulder, then twined his fingers through hers and headed toward the door.

"Where did you park?" Jay asked. Did that hoarse voice belong to him?

She jerked her head toward a parking space right in the front. "There."

That wouldn't do. Too public. "Do you mind if I drive?"

He suspected that under ordinary circumstances he'd get a lecture about having to be in control and how she was perfectly capable of handling a vehicle, but the slight tremor in her fingers revealed that she was every bit as shaken as he was. "Not at all."

She handed him the keys, then looked at him a little funnily when he followed her around to her side of the car and opened the door. "I know you can do it yourself. It's called courtesy."

"I wasn't going to say anything. I'm just not used to it. You're different," she said, a strange note in her voice he couldn't quite decipher. He decided it wasn't an insult, though, and was rather pleased that she thought he was different.

He didn't want to be the same as every other guy she'd met. He wanted to be better. To be the best. To be worthy of her trust and her regard.

What he really wanted, Jay realized, was *her*.

In every sense of the word. Most pressingly at the moment, the biblical sense.

Jay closed the door, rounded the car and then slid behind the wheel. He adjusted the mirrors and seat, then aimed the little sedan into traffic and looked for a secluded area where they could park and he could make her scream. He mentally snorted. Parking? At his age? This was what she'd done to him. What she'd reduced him to.

"Do you know where I'm going?" he asked.

She released a shaky breath. "No, but I wish you'd get there faster."

Jay grinned, spotted an abandoned factory and quickly wheeled the car around to the back of the

building. Not a person in sight. Brilliant. He shoved
the seat back as far as it would go and levered it
down. In the time it took to make sure he could
get his hands on the condom quickly enough, she'd
whipped her shirt over her head and crawled on top of
him. She smelled like green apples and fabric softener
and something else, something that was distinctly
her.

It lit him up.

Her lips found his, soft and skilled and insistent,
her sweet tongue sliding in and out of his mouth.
He mimicked her rhythm with his hips, pushing up
against her. His hands mapped her sleek back, following the fluted hollow of her spine, and he was
struck again at how petite she was—his hands literally spanned her waist.

That enflamed him.

She was small and perfectly made and he wanted
her more than he'd ever wanted anything. She left his
mouth, kissed along her jaw and licked a path over the
rounded muscle of his shoulder, then up and along his
neck. He groped for the clasp on her bra and found
it fortuitously at the front. A quick tug of his fingers
and her breasts were freed, the lacy cups barely clinging to her pearled nipples.

His gaze feasted on her, drank her in, and when
that wasn't enough, he bent forward and pulled a tight
bud into his mouth. She purred for him, a low sibilant
hiss of pleasure that called to his dick like a damned

familiar. It hardened to the point of pain, strained against his zipper and then threatened to mutiny and leave his pants altogether.

And all of this was happening in a car. Like a friggin' teenager with too many hormones and just enough freedom. He should be doing this in a bed, Jay thought dimly, where he'd have more room to taste and sample, explore and savor. Where he could flip her onto her back and dive dick-first into her welcoming heat.

As though telegraphing the thought from his brain to hers, she leaned back and up, then shimmied out of her pants. She didn't bother with the thong.

He'd died and gone to heaven.

Her clothes might be serviceable, but her underwear was downright…sinful. It was red and sheer with a single embroidered rose on the front. He swallowed. Hard.

With more speed than he would have imagined himself capable of while being so distracted, Jay shoved his pants out of the way, drew his dick from his boxers and quickly sheathed himself in a condom.

She moved the thong aside, lifted her hips and slid over him, hissing once more as he nudged her folds. She was wet and hot and heavenly and he'd never seen a more beautiful woman. Smooth skin, pouting breasts, the feminine curve of her hip, the thatch of dark hair nestled over her sex.

Charlie framed his face with her hands, bent forward and kissed him, plunging her tongue into his mouth as she slowly impaled herself on his body.

Only by sheer dint of will did he keep from coming right then.

He was burning up in his own skin, was so hot he thought he was going to burst into flame, much like the fabled phoenix tattooed on his shoulder. She rode him harder, leaning back so that she could take more of him in. Her lips were swollen from his kisses, pink and plump, and her heavily lashed eyes were closed as she enjoyed his body, pleasuring herself in the process.

Charlie approached sex with the same sort of attention to detail, capability and enthusiasm as she did everything else and the payoff resulted in a confident lover who knew what she wanted and how to get it. She was, hands down, the very best partner he'd ever had.

Jay met her thrust for thrust, angling up and deep, looking for that magical spot that would ultimately send her over the edge. Her breathing quickened when he found it, a shallow inhalation that signaled he'd located her sweet spot.

He grinned, took her breast into his mouth and thumbed the other nipple, rolling it lightly between his fingers.

"Jay—" she said, breathless, focused, so damned hot.

"Yes?"

"I think I'm gonna—"

She grunted, mewled, thrashed above him.

"Oh, *yeah*. I'm *definitely*— It's— *Almosssttt...*"

Then she screamed, long and deep, unreservedly.

"I told you I'd make you scream," he said, gratified, self-satisfied and otherwise thrilled.

"That you did," she said, her voice hoarse, stuttering out of her in a sated gasp. She gave him a purely wicked look. "Now I'm going to make you do it."

AT TWENTY-EIGHT YEARS old, Charlie knew she was too old to go parking and should have had enough self-control to wait to take him until they'd at least had the privilege of a bed.

But knowing something and keeping herself from acting on it were two entirely different things.

Her sex still pulsed with the residual climax— the first she hadn't produced solo for the past two years—and the sensation was nothing short of miraculous. She tingled in parts of her body she wasn't aware had nerve endings. He pushed into her, drawing every iota of pleasure from her that he could. He was thrillingly big, amazingly hard and very, *very* well proportioned. Truthfully, the first slide of him into her body had resulted in a near-fainting episode, but she'd clung to him and absorbed the sheer, divine joy of being completely, totally filled.

It was amazing what sort of difference that made. Which made her former lovers sound like they belonged to the Little Dick Club, but in all seriousness it wasn't so much that they'd been small, but that he'd been much more…substantial, Charlie thought as she settled more firmly against him.

"You feel so damned good," he said. "You've been driving me crazy."

He'd been driving her crazy, as well, and then today, when she'd realized that he'd forfeited his own interests to protect an abused girl…

Her heart had simply melted like a dollop of butter over a hot biscuit, and steam had practically oozed from her panties, he'd made her so damned hot.

She hadn't bothered putting up so much as a token protest when he'd pulled the condom from his pants— What had been the point? She'd wanted him. Desperately. Every female portion of her anatomy sang with recognition—with some indefinable something— when he so much as looked at her.

And when he kissed her, when his mouth met hers? Sheer bliss. Unimaginable glory. Utter perfection.

Speaking of which… She leaned forward and found his mouth once more, suckling his bottom lip, drawing it into her own and then slipping her tongue along the plum-soft flesh inside. Another shiver eddied through her and she felt him push deeper into her, felt his big hands slide possessively down over her back, onto her rump, where he gave a light squeeze. Delight barbed through her, tightening her feminine muscles.

She lifted up, dragging his slippery skin with her, then sank slowly back down again, working the long length of him with every bit of her womanly channel. She loved the sleek draw and drag, the delicious friction of their joined bodies. It made her want to go faster and to slow down, left her equally energized and boneless.

She fed at his mouth, tested the angle of his jaw beneath her hands, skimmed the supersoft skin at his temples and felt a pang of emotion land in her chest. She beat it back, determined to keep her heart out of this. To enjoy him, to appreciate him, to celebrate a man who was more honorable than opportunistic, more generous than selfish.

Better.

She rode him harder, upped the rhythm, leaving him no choice but to match her stride, to race for the golden ring of release. Fire licked through her belly and flickered through her sex once more, kindling a powerful, aching throb deep in her womb. He kissed her harder, thrust his tongue into her mouth even as he thrust more thoroughly into her. It was frantic and wild, desperate and dirty, and she liked it, reveled in being out of control, in simply enjoying the basic, fundamental urge to need and be needed.

She felt him tense beneath her, his muscles tighten and strain as the climax built within him. Charlie squeezed around him, rode him with all the strength she possessed, kissed him, licked, nipped and scored his masculine flesh. He bucked wildly beneath her, made guttural masculine sounds that slid like an aphrodisiac into her veins and, though she wouldn't have thought it was possible, made her want him even more.

"Are...you ready?" she breathed.

"Ready for...what?" Harder, faster, then harder still.

"To scream," she told him.

"Sweetheart, I don't scream," he said, his chuckle low and confident.

Charlie reached around and slipped a determined finger over the tautened skin of his balls. The laugh died in his throat as though an off-switch had been thrown, his eyes widened in a instant of shock, and then, gratifyingly...

He screamed.

It was long and primal, more howl, in truth, but the noise she'd been waiting for all the same.

She smiled, gratified, and tightened around him, milking the climax from him one determined squeeze at a time.

Chest heaving, he sagged against the back of the car seat and slung an arm over his forehead. His eyes sparkled with masculine satisfaction and admiration.

"I stand corrected," he said, shooting her an impressed look. "I don't know what you did just then, but... *Damn.*"

Charlie knew the grin on her lips was more than

a little self-satisfied, but she couldn't seem to help it. She leaned forward and pressed a kiss to his mouth, then carefully withdrew and settled back into her own seat. She snagged some tissue from the glove box and handed it to him, then made quick work of righting herself.

She felt *immensely* better. Nothing like a good orgasm to improve one's disposition, Charlie thought, a droll smile curling her lips.

Jay glanced at her, his gaze turning suspicious. "Should I be nervous?"

She laughed at his dubious expression. "Why?"

"Because I don't trust that grin. It's…a little wicked."

"That's because I'm thinking wicked thoughts."

"You should never keep those sorts of thought to yourself, you know," Jay told her, as though imparting a bit of sacred wisdom. "They're better shared."

She grinned. "You mean like worries?"

He shot her a look. "Are worries better shared?"

"They're halved," she said, pulling a one-shouldered shrug. "I guess that would make them better shared. Grief, too."

He frowned, his expression sobering a bit. "Or else it would only make two people depressed as opposed to just the one."

Charlie chuckled softly under her breath, watched as he tucked his shirt back into his pants, then started the car. That sounded personal, but after seeing what he'd done today, she'd be damned before she'd pry. "That's another way of looking at it, Eeyore," she teased.

"Eeyore?" he scoffed, blinking innocently. "What happened to my hero's welcome?"

She smiled and tucked a strand of hair behind her ear. "You just got it."

His grin was pure sin and he sent her a sidelong glance. "I did, didn't I? Have I thanked you yet?"

"Not in the traditional sense, no," Charlie told him. "But I don't feel the least bit slighted." A little sore and sated, primed, aching and strangely terrified, but thoroughly pleasured all the same.

He poked his tongue in his cheek, his eyes twinkling with more masculine satisfaction than was strictly warranted. "I'm glad to hear it." He paused, negotiated a turn and aimed the car toward the Betterworth estate. "I gotta admit I wasn't expecting... that."

Charlie heaved a sigh. "Then that makes two of us." She turned to look at him, drinking him in. "What will you do now?"

He shot her a confused look. "What do you mean?"

"Well, I'm assuming that you're no longer working for Andrew Betterworth," she said. Her lips twitched. "You know, considering that you punched him and he put you in jail."

His jaw tightened and a thundercloud of displeasure suddenly raced across his brow. "It was worth it," he said.

And she knew he meant every word. Charlie swallowed, struck again at how different Jay Weatherford was from any man she'd ever known. Not that she hadn't known good men—she had—but, in her experience, they were a bit thin on the ground. Most of the men she'd known had been so afraid that she was going to outperform them in some way that they hadn't adhered to any sort of principle or code of honor. Her gaze slid to Jay and a peculiar pang tightened in her chest.

Meeting one who did both was as terrifying as it was thrilling.

Quite honestly, she didn't know what to make of him.

He was an unknown quantity, a breed apart from the typical guy. Furthermore, he didn't seem the least bit intimidated by her. Why was that? she wondered now, when she'd managed to frighten so many other men away. It boggled the mind. And miracle of miracles, he seemed to genuinely like and appreciate the very things about her that other men had found worrisome.

"Just because I'm no longer employed by Andrew Betterworth doesn't mean that I'm no longer committed to finding Ms. Aggie's dog," Jay said. "I told her I'd see to it that Truffles was returned to her and

I fully intend to follow through." He darted a look in her direction. "Do you have any objections?"

Not if it meant that he was staying. She shook her head, ridiculously pleased. "None at all."

His vivid eyes rounded in mock surprise, the golden lashes catching the afternoon sun. "Two miracles in one day," he marveled. "This must be a record."

She frowned. "Two miracles?"

"You didn't argue with me and you made me scream." He chuckled darkly and inclined his head. "Those are definitely miracles in my book."

"What would you call it if I made you scream again?" she asked, chewing the inside of her cheek.

He reached over and slid a reverent thumb over her bottom lip. Something elusive shadowed his gaze— wonder, maybe? affection, certainly—and he smiled at her, making her melt all over again.

"Sheer dumb luck," he said. "That's what I'd call it."

He couldn't have answered any better.

_12_

"WHAT ARE YOU GOING to do with her?" Smokey asked as he poked at the ashes. Firelight flickered over his features, illuminating his profile in an orangey glow. His eyelashes were quite long, Aggie noted. How was it that she'd never noticed that before? She'd certainly looked at him often enough.

She sighed, absolutely heartsick over the poor girl upstairs in the Yellow Room. How had things gone so terribly wrong for the child? To think of her living with Andrew, suffering pain and abuse at his hands. It made her mad as hell, made her ache for innocence lost and missed opportunities and the injustices of the world.

"Just love on her a little for now," Aggie told him. She took a sip of her sherry. "Lord knows she needs it."

Everyone needed love. It was a universal requirement, a human desire, occasionally a flaw, but ever present all the same.

Smokey glanced at her over his shoulder, studying her face. "Doesn't sound like the world has been really kind to her."

It hadn't. Horrible parents, opportunistic predators like Andrew. Josie was smart—there was a glimmer of intelligence in her frightened eyes—and there was, miraculously, still a hint of innocence about her despite everything that she'd been through. Those bruises on her legs… Aggie winced, unable to imagine how she'd gotten them. He'd kept her confined without money, without a car, without any means of independence. He'd beaten her down and then promised her the moon. A vicious cycle of hope and disappointment.

Black eyes would heal, bruises would fade, but Aggie almost thought it was the theft of optimism that ultimately was the biggest abuse. Trust was going to be a long time coming, that was for sure.

"Do you think she'll press charges?" Smokey asked.

Aggie chuckled softly. "If Charlie has anything to say about it she will." Her gaze slid to Smokey, who was still crouched in front of the fireplace. He could sit like that forever, she thought. Knees bent, his rear end resting almost on his feet. "I'm so thankful she was here. She's dealt with this sort of thing before and knew exactly what to do." She blinked, still somewhat mystified. "I would never have thought that a bath, of all things, would be the first order of business." She released a soft sigh. "But it was just what she needed."

"You've given her a safe place," Smokey told her. "And the benefit of your kindness. She needed that, as well."

Inexplicably, Aggie felt her eyes burn and water and a little sob rise in her throat.

Smokey looked at her in alarm and frowned, then came and knelt beside her, taking her hand in his.

That only made her cry harder.

He gave a low tsk and peered concernedly into her face. "Aw, come on now," he said, his voice reassuring. "It's not as bad as all that. She's here now. She's safe."

He'd moved closer. The scent of the wood smoke clung to his clothes and swirled up around her. His hand was big and work-worn and the strength in his fingers was thrilling and comforting and Aggie didn't know why she was crying or what it was specifically about Josie's situation that had her emotions all tied up in knots.

She was just…overwhelmed with loss, she supposed. The loss of her friend, the loss of her pet, the loss of a young girl's innocence—her watery gaze slid over Smokey's dear face—the loss of what might have been had she met this man years ago. So much time gone. How different her life would have been had she met the right person to start with. She felt guilty for even thinking it. She'd loved her husband—he'd been a good man—and she'd adored her children. She hadn't had a bad life, and yet...

He reached up and wiped a tear away from beneath her eye with the pad of his thumb, and she closed her eyes and turned her cheek instinctively into his touch. It was bittersweet and wonderful, the warmth of his big hand against her face.

He stilled.

It took more courage than she would have ever imagined to open her eyes and look up at him. She was terrified that she'd crossed an unspoken line, that she'd see regret or misgivings. He was a proud man, she knew that. She was the boss lady with a big bank account and a bigger house and all those other things that men worried over and women didn't give a damn about. He'd said enough over their morning breakfasts for her to glean that much out of him.

His unreadable gaze searched hers, his thumb reverently stroking her cheek. Then, with a soft sigh of supplication and quite deliberately, he reached up and framed her face completely, leaned forward and pressed his lips to hers.

Sensation erupted along her nerve endings and a burst of warmth shot through her veins, bringing anticipation and desire, things she'd imagined weren't a part of her future anymore. She touched his face, as well—how long had she waited to do that, to feel the stubble along his jaw with her hands?—and her chest swelled with an emotion so sweet and pure and powerful that she almost starting weeping again.

When at last he drew back, his eyes were rife with affection and need, with fierce devotion, a mirror of her own, she knew.

And then, of course, there was only one thing left to do.

"Smokey?"

"Yes, Aggie?"

"You're fired."

"WE'VE HEARD FROM Betterworth," Payne told him. "He's threatening to sue us. I told him to go right ahead and we'd see who ran out of money first."

Shit. He'd been afraid of that. He'd been going through his notes, rereading all of the so-called evidence when his boss had called. It didn't matter that Betterworth had fired him—he still felt responsible, still felt there was a key piece of evidence right in front of him that he was missing.

"I'm sorry," Jay told him, passing a hand over his face. "Naturally, I'll cover the legal fees." He had a nice little nest egg socked back. The single life in the military hadn't been a particularly expensive one and he'd come from a family of savers. To his knowledge his dad had never even had a credit card. *Nothing spends better than cash,* he'd always said. Jay smiled, remembering. He'd been planning to use the money to buy a house, but could hardly let the firm pay for his actions.

It suddenly occurred to him that he didn't know where Charlie lived and the thought brought him up short. In fact, there were lots of things he didn't know about her. How odd, when he felt like he'd known her forever, as though a part of him had instinctively recognized her.

"It won't come to that," Payne remarked. "Betterworth is so far in the red it's more maroon. He doesn't have the money to hire a lawyer, much less sue us."

"You've looked at his financials?"

"I pulled them before we ever took him on. He's hanging on by the skin of his teeth." Payne chuckled darkly. "And every bit of his financial future hangs on Truffles. Even if the dog dies a natural death and all the terms of the will are met, Betterworth and that equally lazy sister of his will only inherit a fraction of the fortune." He paused thoughtfully. "I'm not altogether certain that he's smart enough to understand that. The will's quite cleverly worded."

Why in the hell had they taken him on as a client then? Jay wondered. It wasn't as if the company needed the money.

"We should have sent him elsewhere when he called," Payne said. "But on the surface, the report looked like a man who'd gotten a raw deal, who was experiencing cash-flow problems thanks to an eccentric aunt who'd preferred her pet over her family.

It wasn't until I started really digging this morning after you called that I found there was more. A couple of assault and battery charges that had been buried, a few fires, that sort of thing."

Things that Charlie would have found, Jay thought.

"How much, exactly, do Betterworth and the sister inherit if nothing happens to Truffles?"

"A quarter of a million each," Payne said. "And I haven't looked at the sister's financials yet—that's next on my list—but if she's spent the way her brother has then that's not going to keep them out of bankruptcy."

"Would a million each do it?" Jay asked, his spine prickling with unease.

Payne was thoughtful. "Well managed, yes. Do you think—"

"I don't know," Jay told him. "But it seems awfully damned strange, doesn't it?"

"But why not ask for all of it?" Payne argued. "Why only demand less than half?"

"Not to draw suspicion, maybe? Perhaps this first million is all they need to tide them over until the dog passes away. Meanwhile, they'd have some extra money to throw at the attorneys to try and undermine the will."

"It's a thought," Payne said. "But technically…"

"I can't leave," Jay told him. "I'd really like your permission to see this through." He told him about the most recent ransom instructions. "Aggie has gotten

Charlie the equipment she needs to try and hack into the system long enough to see if she can find out who the account belongs to. Provided we don't find out who's taken the dog prior to our next instructions— and frankly, we don't have anything significant to go on and, at this point, I'm not especially hopeful about that—she'll need to be working the hacking angle while I go and get Truffles. She needs me," he said.

The silence on the other end of the line was almost deafening. He'd said too much, Jay realized too late. *Damn, damn, damn.* He winced and passed a hand over his face.

"Permission to stay granted," Payne finally said. He sounded almost…amused?

No doubt Jay would have some explaining to do when he got back, but at least he still had a job and could see this through. "Thank you."

"And Jay?"

"Yes?"

"I'm so glad you nailed that bastard. I can't abide a bully."

And with that parting comment, the line went dead.

Though he hadn't needed their approval to do what he did, Jay was glad to know that he'd had it. More than anything, though, it had been Charlie's reaction to his hotheaded temper that had been the most gratifying.

The look on her face when he'd walked out of the jail...

She'd been so proud of him, for lack of a better description. Those wide autumn-like eyes had been sparkling with more admiration and respect than he'd ever seen before and, though he'd only done what any half-decent man with any sort of character would have done, he got the impression that Charlie hadn't met many of those.

Sad, that.

She was a phenomenal woman. She was smart and funny and droll and was perfectly capable of kicking his ass six ways to Sunday. He chuckled low. Hell, he could admit it. And he didn't mind admitting it. The level of discipline and dedication that went into mastering martial arts was damned admirable. He wasn't going to let a little something like ego get in the way of appreciating her skill.

In fact, it rather turned him on. He liked that she'd speak her mind, that she'd fight her way out of a corner before letting anyone put her there.

He liked *her,* Jay realized in a moment of insight. She'd told him that he was different, but she was the one who was genuinely unique. Remembered heat slid through his limbs and settled in his groin when he thought about what they'd done in her car. *The foggy windows, the shared breaths, her kittenish sounds and the slide of her bare nails over his flesh. The feel of her tight body above his. Dusky nipples,*

creamy flesh, that especially carnal plump bottom lip.
A shiver raced through him and his dick twitched in
his pants.

The next time he had her—and there would definitely be a next time—they were going to do it in a
proper bed, with proper sheets. And he was going to
strip her completely naked and taste every inch of
her bare flesh. He was going to slow things down and
gradually wind her up…and then let her fly.

For a split second Jay considered emailing Payne
and asking him for that background check on her he'd
offered earlier, but ultimately dismissed the idea. If
he wanted to know something, then he'd just ask her,
dammit.

And there was *so* much he wanted to know.

He wanted to know what sort of child she'd been—
he suspected she'd been a little hellcat, of course—
and whether she had any family. He wanted to know
why she'd chosen to go into law enforcement. What
had prompted the career choice in the first place and
why had she left? He wanted to know why she'd applied for the job at Ranger Security and why Juan
Carlos had owed her a favor. He wanted to know
when she'd developed an interest in martial arts and
how long she'd been in training.

He wanted to know her favorite book, her favorite color, her favorite food, if she slept on the right
or left side of the bed, where she lived and whether
she'd ever been seriously involved with someone.

He wanted to know everything about her—every thought, opinion, mole and scar. He grimaced.

The only problem with that was she'd expect the same sort of disclosure in turn. The idea made his blood run cold. She knew the basic facts, of course, thanks to her perusing his file, but she didn't know about the accident.

The explosion, the force of the blast, the heat licking up the back of his legs, the horrible smell of human suffering. Corby McDonald, whom they called Big Hoss, had been on his left, and Matty Upchurch on his right. He'd visited them in the burn unit afterward and… Well, they'd never be the same. Both had "medic'ed out." Corby had a three-year-old and his wife had been pregnant at the time of the accident.

She'd left him.

Matty had gone home to his parents, ordered a suicide kit from a woman in California who'd even offered priority shipping, and ended his own life. Federal agents had since raided the woman's home, but it had been too late for his friend.

One life gone, another ruined…and he'd come out without a blister.

Survivor's guilt, my ass, Jay thought. More like survivor's shame. Survivor's misery. Survivor's agony.

He couldn't face the possibility of anything like that ever happening again, couldn't do the job he'd been trained to do without fear of making a mistake, of jeopardizing his comrades. Of coming away unharmed again and facing the perplexed and envious looks from his friends.

He knew they hadn't blamed him, which was fair because it hadn't been his fault. But they'd resented him.

And that had been worse.

He didn't think he could share that with her. Hadn't shared it with *anybody*.

What was it she'd said? A worry shared was a worry divided? Maybe so, but this was a concern he had to carry himself.

It was the least he could do, really, all things considered.

13

CHARLIE'S EYES WATERED and her back ached, but she was damned pleased with what she'd put together. It had taken her almost the entire night. She glanced at the clock, noting the time, and made a snap decision.

She needed to talk to Jay.

She carefully opened her door, making sure to look for dental floss or any other potential alert he'd rigged, then peeked into the hall. She listened for a moment, satisfied that no one was up yet, then darted across the corridor to his door. He hadn't bothered to lock it, which made her smile. Hopeful she'd turn up? she wondered. Or had he decided not to bother? Either way she was irrationally pleased.

Charlie slipped into the room and scanned the dark bed for his sleeping form. He was sprawled on his side, one leg slung outside the duvet, one beneath, and his arm hung off the edge of the bed. A night-light from the bathroom illuminated the side of his face and it was so relaxed in sleep and so *dear*—dammit, when had that happened?—that it made a lump swell in her throat and her chest squeeze with some troubling, terrifying emotion.

Oh, hell.

This was not good. Not good at all.

Just because he'd decked an asshole and rescued a girl, didn't look at her background check when he'd had the chance, opened doors, admired her intelligence and wasn't threatened by her strength didn't mean she should get…attached to him.

He'd still taken her job.

Granted, he'd abandoned this one in his "official" capacity and had stayed on to help because it was the right thing to do—a man who did the right thing, she marveled wonderingly—but ultimately he still had taken something she'd so desperately wanted.

Working for the Falcon brothers was a fine enough job and she was glad to have it, but she wasn't altogether sure that they had what it took to make it in this business long-term, which meant her job security was less than perfect. How could she consider the possibility of having a family under those circumstances? A year from now she might be unemployed and crawling back to the P.D., her hat in her hands. At the thought of a family, her gaze inexplicably slid to Jay.

No doubt he'd make a great father, she thought, a soft smile curling her lips. He'd be the type of dad

who'd change diapers and embrace his responsibility. He'd be the kind who would get on the floor and
roughhouse with his kids, who wouldn't miss a Little
League game and would help with homework. He'd
instill morals and respect and courtesy and a good
work ethic. He'd be just as proud of a daughter as he
would be of a son and he'd honor her decisions and
not stop talking to her out of petty spite.

She hadn't realized how much that had hurt her
until just now, Charlie thought, scowling. Her father
hadn't behaved like that when Jack had announced
his intentions to follow another path. He'd been disappointed, but at the end of the day he'd clapped him
on the back and all was well.

Why hadn't her dad done that with her? Why had
he made her feel like she was a failure, a second-best
child, a disappointment? Why hadn't he wanted *her*
to be happy? Wasn't that supposed to be a universal
wish for one's children?

In all honesty, though she'd loved her mother,
she'd always thought she had a closer relationship
with her father. They had more shared interests. Her
mother, bless her heart, had never understood her.
Undoubtedly when Charlie was born her mom had
had visions of dresses and matching hair bows and
patent-leather shoes. She grinned. What she'd gotten
was dirty T-shirts, cutoff jeans and sneakers. A girl
who preferred playing baseball to playing house, who
buried her dolls in the dirt so that she could reen-

act a crime scene, one who'd cut off her own hair to keep from having to wear ponytails or those cursed ribbons, a girl who had perpetually skinned knees, broken bones and who got into more fights than her older brother. And won.

She'd been a nightmare, Charlie realized with a slow-dawning smile, suddenly pitying her poor mother.

"I don't know what that smile is for," Jay said, his voice rusty from sleep. "But it's scaring me."

Charlie chuckled and made her way to the bed. She nudged him over so that she could sit on the edge. The spot was warm from his body heat. Nice. "I had to tell you something," she said.

His eyes widened. "You came to *talk?*"

Incredibly, she blushed. She wanted him, too, but the window of opportunity to nail the dognapper was swiftly closing and she needed to focus on work. He was a…distraction. She let her gaze slide over his bare chest, appreciating the muscle and bone, the flat masculine nipples, the sleek skin.

A very, very good one.

"I've been busy."

He glanced at the clock and anxiety suddenly lined his brow. "All night?"

She nodded, unreasonably pleased with his concern. That was new. To her knowledge, other than her mother, no one had ever worried about her. It was an unexpectedly pleasant sensation.

"Sometimes I even amaze myself," she announced just short of a preen. She couldn't help it, dammit. The little program she'd just written was ingenious even if she did say so herself.

And she did.

His eyes brightened with interest. "What have you done?"

"Provided I can get into the system in time, I have just made some computer magic that will move the ransom money immediately back out of the account before they ever realize that it's gone."

Admiration clung to his smile. "Really?"

"Really," she confirmed with a nod. "And the best part? It will look like it's there…until they go to move it."

He peeked at her from beneath lowered lashes. "Is this legal?"

Charlie's cheeks puffed as she exhaled mightily. "Not any part of it."

Smiling, he gave his head a shake. "It utterly amazes me that you used to be a police officer, since you operate with a different set of rules from everyone else."

"I know right from wrong," she said, nodding primly. "But I believe that it's occasionally justified to use so-called wrong means to right a situation." She grimaced. "Spend a little time in a battered women's shelter and you'll see what I mean."

He gave a nod of agreement. "I imagine so." He

paused. "Is that why you went into law enforcement? Because you wanted to right wrongs?"

Charlie felt a wan smile drift over her lips. "Nothing so noble as that," she confided. "Both my grandfather and father are retired police officers." She glanced at him. "You should have read that much on my résumé."

"I didn't read it."

She looked up sharply. "What?"

"I like getting to know you," he said, his frank gaze tangling with hers. "You fascinate me. Every insight is like a little gift. If I'd read it all it would have ruined the surprise."

Wow. As compliments went, she didn't know if she'd ever received anything better. It wasn't a casual remark about her looks or a glib nod to her abilities—it was personal and thoughtful and... Hell, who wouldn't want to be *fascinating?*

Particularly to a man like him.

"Thank you," Charlie demurred, unaccountably nervous.

He grinned at her. "You're blushing."

"Shut up."

"So you decided to follow in your family's footsteps?" he prodded.

"I did. My brother was actually supposed to do it, but he joined the military instead." She shot him a dry look. "He's a Ranger."

Jay chuckled, seemingly enjoying the irony. "Deployed?"

"Afghanistan."

He winced. "Damn. What's his name?"

"Jack Martin."

"The name sounds familiar," Jay told her. "But I can't put a face with it."

"I miss him," she confided, then sighed. "Especially now."

His gaze instantly sharpened. "Why especially now?"

Dammit, she hadn't meant to let that slip. He was too easy to talk to and it was harder to keep her guard up when she was with him. Protecting herself, hiding any perceived weakness had become second nature to her. She also tended to shy away from ultra-feminine clothes—at least the ones that could be seen, anyway—and anything else that might trigger a "weaker sex" mentality in a male coworker.

She'd stopped wearing nail polish when she'd caught a smirk from another officer, but she still loved a pedicure. Her toes were currently painted a deep hunter-green with little fall leaves on them. It gave her a tiny kick of happiness every time she saw them.

Her home was actually where she reveled in her femininity. It was a small Craftsman bungalow she'd decorated with light colors, lots of floral fabric, frilly pillows with fringe and antique dishes and glassware, most of it pink Depression glass. She loved fresh-cut flowers and kept a little vase of them in almost every room. It was her sanctuary and very few people had ever been allowed in.

She'd let Jay in, Charlie realized. And would more than likely never want him to leave.

The thought jarred the answer to his former question out of her. "Because he gets that I wanted to do my own thing," she said. "He backs me up."

Jay frowned, looking perplexed. "Against who? Your family?"

"Just my father. He was very disappointed that I left the P.D." She smiled so it wouldn't sound so bad. "He hasn't spoken to me since I left."

Jay went still. "How long ago did you leave?" His voice was level, but there was an undercurrent of irritation.

She did the math in her head. "About two and a half months ago."

If he was still before, he was like a statue now. Impossibly, he felt hotter. She could feel the heat coming off him in little waves. "Did you anticipate this response?"

Charlie sighed. "I knew he'd be disappointed, but no, I didn't expect him to be so…unmovable."

"I'm sorry," he said, reaching over to take her hand. He threaded his fingers through hers and squeezed. She felt oddly comforted and something else…something darker and more sinful.

"Ah, he'll come around. Eventually," she added. "Are you close to your brother?"

He grinned at her. "You probably remember his name, too, don't you?"

She poked her tongue in her cheek. "Carson. Have you talked to them since they left for Ireland? It was this week, right?"

Lips twitching with humor, he shook his head. "Unbelievable. Yes, they left this week. My mother wants to kiss the Blarney Stone. But to answer your question, no, we're not as close as I'd like to be."

"Pennyroyal isn't that far from Atlanta," she told him. "Maybe you can rectify that."

"That's my goal. Being in the military didn't leave a lot of time for building relationships."

That sounded…significant. Was he, like her, looking for someone? Had a desire for wanting a family of his own sparked his abrupt departure from the military? No, it couldn't have, Charlie realized. He wouldn't have been afraid of her finding that in his file. It wouldn't have sent that blinding flash of fear and shame across his face, the one she still felt guilty for inspiring. Speaking of which…

"I'm sorry I looked through your file, Jay," she said. "At the time you were just my opponent, not a—" She struggled to find the right word, but none seemed to fit.

"—friend," he supplied for her.

She stilled, letting that definition take root. "Special friend," she qualified.

Masculine humor lit his dark gaze and he lowered his voice. "Oooh, I like the sound of that."

He was shameless, Charlie thought. But she secretly liked it. "Had you always wanted to be in the military?" she asked, dipping a pinky toe into more personal territory.

While a wall didn't go up, per se, his expression might as well have posted a friendly no-trespassing sign. "I did," he said. "It was a good career. Making the move to Ranger Security is definitely going to require some adjustment, but ultimately I think it was the right thing for me to do."

He said it by rote, as though this was his standard answer to the question. It wasn't, however, the complete truth. Not based on what she'd seen, anyway. She stared at him for a moment, a silent standoff wherein she let him know that she knew he was lying, and he stared back and didn't elaborate. It stung that he wouldn't confide in her, but ultimately she understood. Whatever it was he was dealing with would have to be done in his own time, in his own way. Admittedly, she was curious and longed to help—to chase away whatever haunted him—but she'd respect the line he'd drawn.

She gave a weak smile, squeezed his hand and jerked her head toward the door. "I'd better get back in my bed," she said.

He essayed a grin, but it wasn't the irreverent one she was used to. A shadow of vulnerability clouded it. "I can scoot over."

She chuckled and dropped her head. She'd just bet he could.

He leaned forward and pressed a kiss to her cheek, his nose sliding along the underside of her jaw. A hard shiver eddied through her and gooseflesh raced across the tops of her thighs. She wanted him—*sweet heaven how she wanted*—but something made her hesitate, some sliver of self-preservation.

Which was utterly ridiculous when she thought about what they'd done yesterday afternoon in the car. Hell, she'd disrobed and straddled him. They'd both *screamed.* It had been wild and frantic, desperate and depraved, and she'd loved every careless, uninhibited second of it.

But intuition told her this time it would be different. This time they weren't just acting on the unprecedented sexual attraction—this time it would *mean* something, and she wasn't sure how her heart was going to feel about that when they went home. Here, they were cocooned in a nice little bubble of their own making. But when they returned to Atlanta and he went back to work for Ranger Security, and she went back to the Falcon brothers, things couldn't stay the same.

And she couldn't afford to let herself fall for someone who needed to keep secrets from her.

Did she respect his privacy? Despite evidence to the contrary, yes. But she wanted a guy who *needed* to tell her his secrets. She wanted to be number one on his speed dial, she wanted to be the first person he called with good news, bad news and the you're-not-going-to-believe-this moments. Too much? Maybe.

But she wouldn't compromise. Couldn't, dammit.

He breathed into her ear, nipped at the lobe. "Don't go, Charlie. Stay with me." His hand framed her face, his fingers sliding almost reverently along her cheek, making pleasure weight her lids, need pool in her sex. "Please."

It was the *please* that did it, because she knew that it cost him. Jay Weatherford wasn't the type of guy who had to say please to get a woman to sleep with him.

He wanted *her.*

And was willing to show her how much by tacking that one entreaty onto the request. It was unequivocally thrilling to be wanted that much, to be desired so thoroughly.

With a bone-deep sigh of supplication—and a certainty of heartache later—Charlie turned her head and kissed him, as well. Lightly, along his brow, his closed eyes, the soft skin at this temple. She rained the kisses delicately over his face, savoring the feel and taste of him.

He growled low in his throat and pulled her down onto the bed with him, lying on his side so that he could stretch her out and enjoy her. He fed at her mouth, long, languid and unhurried kisses that made time irrelevant and her bones turn to mush. He trailed his fingers along the open V of her nightshirt, then slowly started unbuttoning the gown, dipping his head in for a kiss against her flesh with every exposed inch. Every touch was deliberate and designed with her pleasure in mind and so hot it was a miracle her skin didn't burst into flame.

By the time the last button was undone, he was kneeling between her thighs and she was breathing so hard it was embarrassing.

Sweet heaven.

His fingers slipped beneath the minuscule elastic of her thong at her hip and he licked a path along the curve, then across her belly and down the other side. Moisture coated her folds, her nipples were ruched so tight the very air seemed to be too much against them and a sizzling throb had built in her clit.

And he hadn't even touched her there yet.

She whimpered, fisted her hands in the sheets, and it took every bit of willpower she possessed to keep from arching her hips up, begging him for release.

"I think I'll stop now and read a book."

Charlie's eyes widened and her head popped up like a jack-in-the-box. *"What?"* she all but wailed.

He laughed at her, the wretch, then bent forward and blew a long puff of hot air over the swollen nub at the top of her sex. Her neck arching away from the bed, she emitted a low growl and her thighs quaked.

"Jay," she said warningly. "Do *something*."

Another infuriating chuckle. He dipped a finger beneath her panties and slid it along her nether lips. "What do you want me to do, Charlie?"

"Me," she said. "Do *me. Now.*"

He hooked the elastic of her thong and swept the negligible bit of fabric out of the way, then fastened his mouth upon her so fast she gasped sharply and bucked beneath him. He weighted her thighs with his arms, spreading her open, and feasted upon her.

There was no other word for it.

He'd no more than swept his tongue over her clit when she came hard. Little lights danced behind her closed lids, every muscle went rigid with pleasure— the equivalent of a standing ovation in her body—and the breath that she'd just sucked into her lungs was held hostage until the orgasm crested and she could release it.

He reached up and massaged her breast and then his mouth followed his hand and he worked the budded crown against his tongue, sucking hard. Meanwhile, he was dallying between her legs again, thumbing her clit while laving her nipple, and, impossibly, she felt release building again. The dual assault was purposeful and relentless and there seemed to be a magical thread running between the two sensitive areas because every lick or stroke of the one elicited a similar response in the other.

"Jay, please," she said, her turn to entreat. Sweat slicked her brow and her skin burned and need coiled tighter and tighter, bending her to its will.

Though she didn't know where it had come from or how he'd gotten it on without her noticing, Jay was suddenly sheathed in a condom and poised between her legs, nudging her entrance.

Breathing heavily, desperate for him, she looked up and the image he made would no doubt forever be burned into her memory. He was absolutely glorious. Curly lashes drooping low over his heavy-lidded eyes, the fine line of his shoulder as it elongated into his muscled arms, his chest a masculine work of art. He was splendidly made, Charlie thought.

And for the moment, *hers.*

Feeling an undeniable surge of possessiveness, she lifted her hips and rubbed herself against him, sucked a harsh breath between her teeth as pleasure bloomed through her, then scored his chest lightly with her fingernails.

As though she'd flipped some sort of unseen switch, he set his jaw and plunged into her, seating himself to the hilt. A fleeting expression raced across his face too fast for her to translate, but whatever it was triggered an almost primal response in him.

His lips peeled away from his teeth, a guttural growl tore from his throat and he clasped her hips, lifted her off the mattress and plunged into her repeatedly. It was hot and hard and frantic and, unlike the marathon of evenly paced foreplay, this was a sprint that he was determined to win.

He took her as if the hounds of hell were riding his ass, and if he looked back or stopped for a breath, he'd surely die.

Fine, Charlie thought. *I'll run with him.* She anchored her legs around his back and matched his rhythm, tightening her feminine muscles around him as he withdrew, trying to hold on to him, to keep him inside her. She clung to him, held him as close as she could, her nipples abrading his chest with each frenzied thrust. She licked his neck, sucked his shoulder, ran her hands all over his body, relishing the feel of his hot skin beneath her greedy palms. She loved the way he felt, how he made *her* feel—desired and special, mysterious and unique. As if she was the most interesting thing in his world, and when he was with her, she was all that existed.

Heady stuff, that.

He pushed harder, his breathing ragged. His tight balls slapped at her sensitive flesh as he hammered into her, a pleasant sting that accompanied his every thrust.

The orgasm caught her completely unaware—one moment she was determined to hold on to him, to keep running this insane race—and the next she was free-falling through sensation, high on utter bliss.

Her heart expanded so much in her chest she felt it lodge in her throat, and the emotion that came with it was bittersweet and so extraordinary it made her eyes water.

It didn't matter if she never saw him again after this was over, Charlie thought. He'd always have a piece of her...whether he wanted it or not.

HE'D WANTED HER ENOUGH to say please, Jay thought as Charlie's tight body clung and fisted around his. That should have been warning enough, should have tipped him off that he'd waded too far in over his head.

But that was the thing about drowning, wasn't it? A person didn't realize it was happening until it was too damned late.

She kissed his shoulder, her hot mouth sliding over his skin, downy soft and moist. Honestly, did she have any idea what she was doing to him? How she'd somehow managed to make him beg to bed her when he'd only ever used *please* as a courtesy, never as a plea?

She'd hesitated, he knew. He'd been able to feel it, sensed it even. But he'd had to make her want him, he'd had to win, and now, too late, he knew why she'd tried to hold her ground.

Because the minute he'd pushed inside her again, his own ground had abruptly vanished from beneath his feet.

Everything had shifted. Whatever it was between

them had gone from being hot and insane to equally hot but emotionally compromised. With every frantic, frenzied thrust into her welcoming body he felt the bond between them strengthening, his desire to claim and protect pushing everything else out of the way. Good sense, reason, logic.

None of that mattered.

Only her. Only how she made him feel.

Honestly, he'd thought if he focused more on the sex—on bringing her release—he'd be able to flee the inescapable truth bearing down on him.

She wasn't just his "special friend," as she'd said… she was *special*.

Unique, matchless, rare.

And though he couldn't have met her at a more inopportune moment, he grimly suspected that he was going to have to have her.

Permanently.

The thought had no sooner flitted through his mind when release claimed him. He buried his toes into the mattress, lifted her up and dived deep, lodging himself as far into her as he could. His vision clouded, blackened, then refocused in Technicolor. He shuddered as sensation rocketed through him, leaving him weak and sated and undeniably hers.

And for the first time in his life, truly vulnerable.

He didn't like that one damned bit.

14

CHARLIE WAS ALMOST thankful that everything went to hell in a handbasket mere minutes after she'd made it to her own room. Aggie roused the house with news that she'd received the first text message from the dognappers. It wasn't the first digits of the account number as expected, but a time-stamped thirty-second-long video of Truffles.

"She's alive!" Aggie cried, her face wreathed in a smile, her eyes watering with joy.

She was indeed, Charlie thought. It couldn't be anything short of healthy to be arched up like that, making her contribution to fertilizing the earth, could it?

Jay grimaced comically, his expression a far cry from the sleepy-eyed look of sexual happiness she'd seen only minutes before. "Is it—"

"Yes," Charlie confirmed. "It is."

"Gross," Jasmine said, peering over Aggie's shoulder. "Oh, God! Look! She's running around like she's won the Doggy Poop of the Year Award or something."

"She's always done that," Aggie said fondly, her throat sounding choked. "It's charming, isn't it?"

Yes, Charlie thought. The little dog was nothing short of adorable. She and Jay shared a look and he made a quick grimace of disgust then gave his head a shake, as though the happy dance didn't make up for the fact that they'd just watched a dog poop. It was all she could do not to laugh. He suddenly stilled, his attention diverted to the lettering on the back of Jasmine's T-shirt. She felt him go on point, completely alert, and his gaze swung immediately back to hers. He glanced significantly at her, then cleared his throat.

"The Pancake Palace and Tattoo Parlor?" Jay remarked, laughing. "That's an interesting combination."

Jasmine smiled up at him, blatantly flirting. "It's an interesting place."

He played along. A little too well if you asked Charlie. "Want to see my ink?"

At Jasmine's nod, he lifted the sleeve of his shirt, revealing an orange and red bird rising out of a nest of flames. It was beautifully done, eminently significant—he wouldn't have put it on his body otherwise—and she didn't know how on earth she'd missed it.

"It's a phoenix," he said.

"It looks new," Jasmine remarked, sounding impressed.

His gaze skittered to Charlie's, then darted away. "It is. I've only had it a few months. What about you? Have you got any ink?"

She turned and lifted the hem of her shirt to reveal two crossed fishhooks along with a man's name and dates of birth and death.

Her father, Charlie realized. The shirt, the bobber, an unobstructed view of the backyard. In a nanosecond she realized why the block letters on the ransom note had been niggling at her—some of them had been cut out from the pamphlet that Burt had given her.

Charlie didn't know why—though she'd find out soon enough—but Jasmine had definitely had something to do with taking Truffles.

"William Harris," Jay read, shooting Jasmine a questioning look.

"He was my father."

Jay winced. "I'm sorry for your loss."

"It's all right," she said. "Burt's kind of taken me under his wing."

So she'd kidnapped the dog for Burt? Because she thought he'd been slighted by Marigold? But why ask for so much?

Fuck it, Charlie thought. She knew where to get the answers. Though she didn't think she'd telegraphed her intent, Jay gave Aggie a little nudge out of the way, leaving a better path for the kick she abruptly swept in Jasmine's direction.

The girl dropped like a stone, the breath whooshing out of her as her back hit the kitchen floor. Smokey stood so fast his chair fell, Aggie screamed and put a hand to her throat and Jay put himself between Jasmine and the door.

Charlie dropped to her knees, straddling Jasmine, and grabbed her wrist until she screamed. "Listen to me," Charlie told her, her tone lethal. "You are going to get one opportunity to tell me the truth—just one," she emphasized. "And if you don't do it I'm going to hurt you in ways you've never imagined. Do I make myself clear?"

Jasmine's panicked gaze darted around the kitchen. "Get her off of me! She's attacking me!"

"No, I'm subduing you," Charlie told her. She smiled without humor. "You'll know when I attack. Where's Truffles?"

Jasmine whimpered, looked away. "I don't know."

Charlie applied more pressure.

"I don't know!" she screamed, thrashing wildly. "Really! I gave her to Andrew! He's g-got her," she sobbed.

She and Jay shared a look. "Did you see any evidence of the dog when you were over there?"

"No, but he would have hidden it, wouldn't he?"

Unshed tears sparkled in Aggie's eyes. "Why, Jasmine? Why would you do such a thing?"

"I did it for Burt," she said, glaring darkly at the older woman. "It wasn't right that the rest of you had benefited so much and he was excluded just because he was a little different. What would it have mattered if he'd given the whole lot of it to his UFO club? It should have been *his* reward to do with as he pleased. Andrew promised to make it right if I took Truffles. Fair is fair."

"That's right," Charlie told her. "Did Burt ever tell you that Goldie Betterworth bought him his house?"

Jasmine blinked. "What? But that's not—"

"She did," Aggie confirmed sadly. "Goldie rewarded everyone who had served her well, who'd worked hard and was worthy. The only people she excluded were the lazy, entitled ones who were more interested in frittering away their legacy than preserving it."

Jasmine shook her head. "But that's not— Andrew told me—"

"What did Burt tell you?" Jay asked.

"Nothing," she said dully. "He never complained."

"That's because he didn't have a reason to," Charlie told her.

Seemingly oblivious to the scene in the kitchen, Josie strolled in and immediately went to stand by Aggie's side. She looked down at the phone and smiled. "Aw, that looks just like Taffy's dog."

"Andrew's sister's dog?" Jay asked. "Isn't Taffy out of the country?"

Josie nodded. "She is, but her housekeeper is home. Rosalind is taking care of her while Taffy's away."

"How do you know this?" Aggie asked her.

"Andrew told me. We had to drop some toys by there day before yesterday." She winced. "Evidently she'd been chewing up all the corners of the rugs."

"And you saw her?" Jay asked. "You're certain this is the dog?"

Josie hesitated. "As sure as I can be with only seeing her for a few minutes. Her nails were painted pink and had little blings attached to them." She grinned. "It was so cute."

Both Jay and Charlie looked at Aggie, who was so overwrought she couldn't speak, but nodded in confirmation. Smokey had moved up behind her, his hand placed protectively on the small of her back. The sight made a lump swell in Charlie's throat. Ill-timed, but there all the same.

Just then Aggie's phone chirped with a new message.

The first of the routing numbers had arrived.

JAY LEAPED INTO ACTION. "Charlie, go work your computer magic." Without a moment's hesitation, Charlie snatched the cell phone from Aggie's hand and raced from the room.

"Smokey, can you see to—"

Smokey jerked Jasmine up by the arm and propelled her to a chair. "I'll watch her."

Jay looked at Josie. "Can you get me back to Taffy's?"

She nodded.

A thought struck. "Are you afraid? If so, you can give me directions and I'll—"

"I'll be fine," Josie assured him with a smile. "Charlie taught me a few things."

"Then let's go." He made for the door. "Aggie, you keep me posted on what's happening here. We can't be sure that he hasn't moved the dog, but on the off chance that she's still at Taffy's I want the element of surprise."

Aggie nodded and stiffened her spine. She sent a dark look at Jasmine, who quailed beneath that ominous stare. "Meanwhile, I'm going to call the police," Aggie said. "*No one* messes with my dog and gets away with it."

Smokey glanced at Jasmine, who'd begun to cry. "She's a sweet woman," he told her. "But there's no worse place to be than on her bad side."

Jay barely caught Smokey's last remark and laughed softly under his breath. He imagined that was a true enough adage for *all* women.

He'd no sooner squealed out of the driveway before his cell phone rang. "She's not going to be there,"

Aggie told him. "I just got a message that he's going to leave her in the park on Calhoun Street. It's—"

"I know where it is," Jay told her. "I passed it on my way in."

"Hurry, Jay," she fretted. "I'd hate for someone else to take her because we were too late." He sped up, hitting the accelerator hard.

"How's Charlie doing?"

A pause, then, "She's typing fast and mumbling under her breath."

Atta girl, Jay thought, his diabolical little master hacker. "I'm going to the park," he said. "Don't worry, Aggie." He disconnected and nudged the speedometer higher.

"You're going to get a ticket," Josie remarked, with a white-knuckled grip on the seat.

"Close your eyes," he suggested. "It'll make you feel better."

"Yep," she agreed grimly. "All the way to the scene of the crash."

A startled laugh stuttered out of his throat. With that sort of sense of humor, he was confident that Josie Miller was going to be just fine. He negotiated a tight turn, passed a car that was going too slowly and narrowly missed a squirrel.

His cell rang again, but this time it was Smokey. "Come back," he said. "Jasmine just told us he's going to put the dog back into the yard the same way that she got it out—with a fishing pole and a net."

Jay stomped on the brake, did an illegal U-turn and hurried back in the other direction.

Josie turned green and clamped her hand over her mouth. "I think I'm going to be sick."

Jay looked over and a couple of puckered marks on her hand caught his attention. "What happened to your hand?" he asked. He knew what it looked like, but...

She blinked. "Oh. Andrew had a thing for fire," she said. Her voice hardened. "I was his favorite thing to burn."

Jesus. And that psychopath was going to deliver the dog to the house? But why? Why would he take such a risk? Why would he hazard getting that close to being caught?

Jay's cell rang, but before he could answer it the sound of a siren blared behind him and then a fire truck sped past.

His heart dropped to his feet.

Oh, no. No, no, no.

Josie gasped, spying the smoke from down the street about the same time he did. Hands shaking, his stomach full of lead and dread, he hurtled down the drive, shoved the gearshift into Park and darted from the car, leaving the door open and the engine running. Aggie, with tears streaming and the dog clutched to her chest, Smokey, Jasmine and Burt were all outside on the front lawn. Burt had Andrew pinned to the ground.

Charlie was nowhere to be seen.

He slowed as he neared them. "Where's Charlie?"

"She's in there," Smokey told him, his eyes full of regret. "He threw it right into the library. A Molotov cocktail."

Jay barely heard him, the blood was pounding in his ears so hard. He darted past one fireman and was almost in the door when another snagged him by the arm. "Hey, buddy, you can't go in there."

Jay violently shrugged him off and darted through the door. Flames licked up the sides of the walls and curled around the ceiling, the smoke so thick it burned his eyes and scalded his throat. "Charlie!" he screamed, desperate to find her. "Charlie!" He dropped down onto his belly and crawled to the library, choking on the thick smoke, feeling the heat roll down on his back.

Not her, not her, not her.

He couldn't bear it if she—

He couldn't even think it. Closed his mind down to the possibility of anything but a perfect, smiling Charlie, his Kitty-Cat, and focused solely on finding her. The fire blazed higher at the back of the library, which was where she'd set up. She said she'd liked the view better.

No, no, no...

"Charlie!"

He kept crawling into furniture and over bits of broken glass, but he pushed on. He had to find her.

Couldn't let it get her, too. Couldn't fail her as he'd failed his friends. He—

Jay spied her hand beneath the desk and relief poured through him. He scrambled forward, grabbed her and pulled her toward him. She was limp as a dishrag. "Charlie!"

Nothing.

No, no, no...

He gathered her up, then stood and raced through the smoke and flames back the way he'd come. He barreled out the front door, dropped to his knees in the cool grass and screamed for help.

Or at least he tried. No sound emerged from his mouth. He was afraid to look down at her, afraid of what he'd see.

And that was the last thought he had before collapsing.

15

CHARLIE AWOKE TO THE sound of various beeping noises, the feel of scratchy sheets against her cheek and the strong scent of antiseptic cleaner.

"Now you've done gone and woken her up," a male voice she vaguely recognized complained.

She pushed up from the hospital bed, her hand still firmly around Jay's, and looked toward the door.

Brian Payne, Jamie Flanagan and Guy McCann stood just inside the room.

"We came to relieve you," Payne told her. "You need to rest."

They'd had this conversation before already and she won every time. She didn't know why they kept bothering. "I'll rest when he wakes up."

She turned away from them, gazed at Jay, tracing the woefully familiar lines of his face. Other than a few blisters around his mouth and his cracked lips, one would never know that he'd been in a terrible fire. His right arm—his shoulder, specifically—was another matter altogether.

His phoenix was gone.

"We brought backup this time," Jamie told her.

She didn't bother to turn around. "It doesn't matter if you brought the friggin' National Guard. I'm not leaving."

"Charlie," a familiar voice said.

She gasped and whirled. "Juan Carlos! I thought you were on vacation!"

"I was," he said, opening his arms. "But the Atlantic Ocean isn't going anywhere and I heard you might need me."

Tears burned the backs of Charlie's eyes and she launched herself at him, more grateful than she could ever imagine to see her friend. Sobs wrenched from her still-raw throat and she relived the horror of the past forty-eight hours.

Waking up in the ambulance, catching enough of the medical speak to know that Jay had been seriously injured. Finding out that he'd barged recklessly into a burning building to save her.

And then being told by Payne why that was so significant.

When the hospital had requested his previous medical records, evidence of the last fire was contained in them. A few well-placed calls had yielded a horrible story that no man should have to live with. The ruined life of one friend, the suicide of another...

Her heart broke for him. And she'd never, *never* ask him to share that with her.

Juan Carlos stroked her back. "He's going to be all right, Charlie," he soothed. "He ate a lot of smoke, yes, but Payne tells me the doctors assured him that Jay will make a full recovery." He chuckled. "And they know better than to lie to him. The maternity ward is named for him, after all."

Charlie pulled back and gave him a watery smile. "It is?"

"Payne wanted better state-of-the-art care when his next child was born."

She blinked. "Oh."

He studied the smudges beneath her eyes and tsked under his breath. "You need to rest. His family should be here soon."

She shook her head. "They're trapped in Ireland. That volcano in Iceland erupted again and the ash is limiting visibility."

"Nevertheless, you're dead on your feet."

Her eyes watered again. "And he almost died. For me. I'm not leaving."

Juan Carlos turned and looked at his employers, then gave a helpless shrug. "I told you she was stubborn."

Jamie swallowed. "I think I'd call that loyal."

"At least let me get you something to eat."

"I'm not hungry—" the idea of food made her stomach heave "—but a drink would be nice."

"You want some alcohol in it? A little something to take the edge off?" he cajoled.

She smiled wanly and shook her head. "Just a soda would be fine."

Juan Carlos nodded. "You got it, sweetheart. I'll be right back."

When he left, Payne gestured for the other two to leave the room, as well. He walked to the window and looked out over the city, clasped his hands behind his back. "Do you know that I've been wrong more in the past week than I have been in the past decade?"

She chuckled tiredly and resumed her vigil by Jay's bed. "Then you're still right a hell of a lot more than the rest of us."

"Be that as it may, it's been quite…humbling." He shot her a smile over his shoulder. "According to my wife, I needed it."

She grunted. "Sounds like a smart woman."

"She is," Payne told her, affection lacing his voice. "You actually remind me of her. You both have that same sort of pluck, determination."

He'd married someone like her? Charlie thought, amazed. She'd pegged him for a king-of-his-castle kind of guy with a wife who deferred to him and made him feel even smarter than he already was.

Hmm. It looked as though she could be wrong, as well.

"I was wrong not to hire you," Payne said. "You

are a first-class agent who would make a fine addition to any team. I'd like you on mine."

Charlie blinked, surprised. He couldn't have shocked her any more if he'd been trying. Honestly, since Jay had been hurt she hadn't given a thought to any job…even the dream one she'd been so certain she wanted.

"You don't have to answer now," he said. "Just think about it."

She nodded, unsure of what to say. He hesitated, seemed on the verge of saying more, then evidently thought better of it and turned to go.

"You said you'd made two mistakes," Charlie reminded him. "What was the other one?"

He grinned. "Not warning Jay about you," he said. "Not that it would have done any good, but…" He shrugged a goodbye and then ducked out the door.

Done any good? Charlie thought. What did he mean by that? Exhausted, she laid her head against the back of Jay's hand and drifted off to sleep once more.

After all, she was going to need her strength to kill him when he woke up.

JAY BECAME AWARE OF his surroundings a degree at a time. He blinked, his eyes gritty and dry, but didn't have any luck bringing the world into focus. He could hear a machine dinging next to him, felt something over his mouth and noted the air tasted funny.

Probably because his mouth was parched, he decided, more thirsty than he'd ever been in his life. A hand held his—soft and small—and the scent of green apples slid into his nostrils.

Charlie! Panic punched him in the gut and he sat bolt upright, tearing the thing off his face, swinging his feet over the side of the bed.

"Jay!" she said, her voice strained but recognizable. She gently pushed him back down and shushed him. "It's okay," she soothed. "You're going to be all right." Her voice broke at the end and she buried her face in his neck, put her arms around him and held him close.

The fire, Charlie… He remembered getting her out, remembered being afraid to look at her.

"Charlie," he rasped. "You…okay?"

"Shush," she said. "Don't try to talk. Your throat is burned. And yes, I'm o-okay."

She didn't sound okay—she sounded like she was crying.

He rubbed his eyes, making another attempt to see. He blinked and the room slowly appeared, fuzzy at first, but clearer by the second.

He drew back to look at her. Her eyes were puffy and red, the lashes clumped together as though she'd been crying a lot. There was a bruise on her cheek, a scratch on her forehead, but otherwise she appeared perfect.

The relieved breath that eased out of his lungs hurt

more than he expected, but it was worth it. He smiled down at her, slid a finger along her cheek. "Kill… Andrew for…hurting you," he rasped.

She chuckled softly and shook her head. "I'm going to kill you for going into that damned library," she said. "There were firemen there! In special little suits designed to keep them from burning to death! You should have let them handle it, damn you." Her face crumpled into a sob. "You shouldn't have risked it, not after…not after Baghdad."

He should have known that she'd find out the truth one way or another and was too relieved that she was okay to consider being angry. He'd been so frightened, so terrified that something had happened to her. That she'd been hurt.

It had put everything else into perspective.

At some point over the last few days, Charlie Martin had become his gravity, the thing that tied him to this world, and though he didn't understand it—wasn't even sure he altogether liked it, for that matter—he couldn't deny it.

How bizarre that it had taken a girl who could cut him off at the knees to be what ultimately grounded him.

He drew her to him, savored the feel of her nestled in his arms. "It's…all right," he said. "I…had to save…you. I…couldn't bear it…if…"

She pulled back and looked up at him. "I would have done the same thing for you," she said. "And then you'd be the one lecturing me for reckless behavior." Her gaze softened. "But that's what heroes do, isn't it? And you're mine."

"I'm…going to…quit my job," he rasped.

Her eyes widened.

"What? Why?"

"Because I can't…work for men…who underestimate you." And he couldn't. She was brilliant. She was brave. She was strong. She was…wonderful. Everything he'd never known he wanted. And more.

Her eyes sparkled with unshed tears and she trailed her fingers lovingly over his face. "Well, you can't quit," she said. "I've told them that we're going to share your apartment instead of me getting my own in the building when I come to work for them." She bit her lip. "I figure we'll have more opportunity to make each other scream if we're cohabitating." She peeked at him from beneath lowered lashes. "Does that work for you?"

"That depends. Are you willing…to make…an honest man…of me?"

She beamed at him, her heart in her eyes. "I'll wheel you down to the hospital chapel right now if that's what you want."

Jay laughed, though it hurt, and shook his head. Oh, no. He wanted the whole shebang. "White dress. Flowers. Parents. Friends. Honeymoon." He squeezed her hand, swallowed so that he could say it without pausing. "I love you, Charlie. When I thought…" He shook his head and shrugged helplessly and knew he wouldn't have been able to finish the sentence even if his throat hadn't been so damned raw.

A tear spilled down her cheek. "I love you, too, Jay. So much that it scares me," she admitted, as though it was a mortifying weakness.

"Then we can be…terrified together. And that's damned sure…better than…apart."

"I can't argue with that," she said. Her hazel eyes glimmered with humor and she tucked her chin against her chest as though imparting a conspiratorial secret. "And we both know I would if I could."

"True enough." He laughed silently and shook his head.

He was marrying this wonderful creature, Jay thought with equal parts joy and awe. She was going to be his.

His.

All because of Truffles the Yorkie.

Epilogue

One month later...

"LOOK AT THEM," Aggie whispered, nodding her head in Jay and Charlie's direction. "He can't take his eyes off her."

Smokey knew the feeling. "She makes a very fine bride."

And it was true. Charlie's dark hair had been swept up in an arrangement of soft curls and the dress she was wearing had belonged to her mother. For reasons that had been kept private, she'd broken with tradition and had her grandfather and brother give her away. Her father had missed the wedding, but had arrived later, with a bit of feet shuffling and a shamed face, at the reception. He'd spoken to the bride and groom and, though Smokey had been afraid there for a moment that Jay was going to be throwing another punch that might end with him incarcerated again, ultimately it had ended fine.

Everything had, really.

Truffles had been returned safe and sound, Josie had taken Jasmine's place and gone to work for Aggie—and was currently enrolled at the local community college on "scholarship." Burt—who'd had no clue that everything that had happened was as a direct result of Jasmine feeling he'd been slighted—was manning his station at the front gate, still searching the skies for UFOs, of course, and Taffy and Andrew Betterworth were in jail, unable to make bond. Jay and Charlie had survived the fire and were now married, and Aggie had done Smokey himself the greatest kindness by firing him so that he could court her properly without feeling weird about it.

Which was just as well, because he was about to propose to her.

He was as nervous as a cat in a room full of rocking chairs.

"Aggie, would you walk with me?"

She smiled up at him and threaded her fingers through his. "Of course."

"Have you ever been to Cade's Cove?" he asked.

Her eyes lit with warmth and nodded. "Once," she said. "Many years ago."

"It's my favorite part of the Smokey Mountains," he said. "It's peaceful, serene, and the wildlife thrives there, more so than in any other part of the park."

They strolled into the church parlor and he led her over to a little Queen Anne sofa. "Really?" she said. "I didn't know that. This is a lovely room," she remarked, looking around. "How did you know this was here?"

"I saw it earlier," he told her. Only because he'd gone looking for it. He'd wanted a quiet place to make his plea. "Anyway, there's a white clapboard church over there that's still in service today."

"I had no idea."

He slid down onto one knee in front of her and pulled the ring from his pocket. "How would you feel about marrying me there?"

Aggie's mouth rounded in a silent O and she looked from him to the ring then back again. "Y-you want to marry me?" she repeated.

He grinned up at her, took her hand and slipped the diamond over her left knuckle and into place. *"Fervently."*

Aggie placed both hands on his face and drew him to her for a kiss. She smiled against his lips. "If I'd known the way to get you to propose was to fire you, I'd have done it a long time ago."

"It's a shame I don't know how to be insubordinate," he teased.

"That's because you're a good man, Smokey Burkhart, and it'll be an honor to be your wife."

And it would be an honor to be her husband.

* * * * *

PASSION

For a spicier, decidedly hotter read—
this is your destination for romance!

COMING NEXT MONTH
AVAILABLE JANUARY 31, 2012

#663 ONCE UPON A VALENTINE
Bedtime Stories
Stephanie Bond, Leslie Kelly, Michelle Rowen

#664 THE KEEPER
Men Out of Uniform
Rhonda Nelson

#665 CHOOSE ME
It's Trading Men!
Jo Leigh

#666 SEX, LIES AND VALENTINES
Undercover Operatives
Tawny Weber

#667 BRING IT ON
Island Nights
Kira Sinclair

#668 THE PLAYER'S CLUB: LINCOLN
The Player's Club
Cathy Yardley

REQUEST YOUR FREE BOOKS!
2 FREE NOVELS PLUS 2 FREE GIFTS!

red-hot reads!

Rhonda Nelson

SIZZLES WITH ANOTHER INSTALLMENT OF

When former ranger Jack Martin is assigned to
provide security to Mariette Levine, a local pastry
chef, he believes this will be an open-and-shut case.
Yet the danger becomes all too real when Mariette is
attacked. But things aren't always what they seem,
and soon Jack's protective instincts demand he save
the woman he is quickly falling for.

THE KEEPER

**Available February 2012
wherever books are sold.**

*Louisa Morgan loves being around children.
So when she has the opportunity to tutor bedridden Ellie,
she's determined to bring joy back into the motherless
girl's world. Can she also help Ellie's father open his
heart again? Read on for a sneak peek of*

THE COWBOY FATHER

*by Linda Ford,
available February 2012 from Love Inspired Historical.*

Why had Louisa thought she could do this job? A bubble of self-pity whispered she was totally useless, but Louisa ignored it. She wasn't useless. She could help Ellie if the child allowed it.

Emmet walked her out, waiting until they were out of earshot to speak. "I sense you and Ellie are not getting along."

"Ellie has lost her freedom. On top of that, everything is new. Familiar things are gone. Her only defense is to exert what little independence she has left. I believe she will soon tire of it and find there are more enjoyable ways to pass the time."

He looked doubtful. Louisa feared he would tell her not to return. But after several seconds' consideration, he sighed heavily. "You're right about one thing. She's lost everything. She can hardly be blamed for feeling out of sorts."

"She hasn't lost everything, though." Her words were quiet, coming from a place full of certainty that Emmet was more than enough for this child. "She has you."

"She'll always have me. As long as I live." He clenched his fists. "And I fully intend to raise her in such a way that even if something happened to me, she would never feel like I was gone. I'd be in her thoughts and in her actions every day."

Peace filled Louisa. "Exactly what my father did."

Their gazes connected, forged a single thought about fathers and daughters...how each needed the other. How sweet the relationship was.

Louisa tipped her head away first. "I'll see you tomorrow."

Emmet nodded. "Until tomorrow then."

She climbed behind the wheel of their automobile and turned toward home. She admired Emmet's devotion to his child. It reminded her of the love her own father had lavished on Louisa and her sisters. Louisa smiled as fond memories of her father filled her thoughts. Ellie was a fortunate child to know such love.

Louisa understands what both father and daughter are going through. Will her compassion help them heal—and form a new family? Find out in
THE COWBOY FATHER
by Linda Ford, available February 14, 2012.

Love Inspired Books celebrates 15 years of inspirational romance in 2012! February puts the spotlight on Love Inspired Historical, with each book celebrating family and the special place it has in our hearts. Be sure to pick up all four Love Inspired Historical stories, available February 14, wherever books are sold.

SHLIHEXP0212

USA TODAY bestselling author

Sarah Morgan

brings readers another enchanting story

ONCE A FERRARA WIFE...

When Laurel Ferrara is summoned back to Sicily
by her estranged husband, billionaire
Cristiano Ferrara, Laurel knows things are about
to heat up. And Cristiano's power is a potent
reminder of his Sicilian dynasty's unbreakable rule:
once a Ferrara wife, always a Ferrara wife....

Sparks fly this February